AZALEA FERN

AND THE LAST RUIN OF THE EXTINCT

BECCI MURRAY

Llama House Children's Books

With huge thanks to
Jacob Smith
for being the very first person to read this book

ISBN: 978-1-913944-11-7

Published by Llama House Children's Books

For my big sister, Joanne

1968 - 2000

CONTENTS

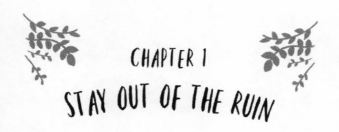

CHAPTER 1
STAY OUT OF THE RUIN

The mechanicary house was warm but damp, the mould and moss of a thousand seasons crumbling the remains of the brickwork. From within the darkness, a roosting crow-hen called without warning. It startled the old building and a shower of dust rained down on the children, lacing their shoulders with ghosts of the past.

The boy wrapped his arms tight around his body, shielding himself from whatever still lingered in the ancient air, but excitement slid down the girl's spine like a wet bull-toad.

"Do you reckon the mechanicary's big?" she asked, peering into the overgrown stairwell in the back wall. "I reckon it's the size of a whale, maybe bigger. Just think, an *actual* mechanicary right under our very feet."

"We shouldn't be here," he said. "It don't feel right."

A crunch of gravel from outside the building made the boy snatch hold of her hand.

The door creaked. A sharp blade of sunlight cut through the darkness. It slipped across the floor like a death-adder, stopping just short of their feet as a silhouette appeared in the doorway. It was a Homotium, a female, and she ducked beneath the ivy-entangled frame, sniffing the air like a sand-fox.

The children froze, hardly daring to breathe, as the girl remembered the words of her mother. "Stay out of the ruin. *Stay out* of the ruin." Then the figure snarled and her eyes blazed suddenly silver, blinding them both in her dazzling light, as the girl let go of his hand and cried, "*Run!*"

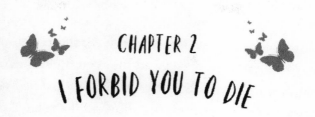

CHAPTER 2
I FORBID YOU TO DIE

Azalea Fern dived fully-clothed into the warm pool without so much as a ripple, resurfaced, then pushed her thick, tangled hair back off her face. Her friend, a short round boy with beautifully freckled skin, pulled a face as if chewing a hornet-bees' nest.

"I en't playing," he said. "What's the point when I never win?"

The water shone like a well-polished diamond. It glistened in the beating sunlight, nestled amongst lush fern trees and bright marsh flowers. Springtime was the best season for swimming: summer was too hot to do anything, autumn was a time for harvesting and when winter arrived the pool became frozen from top to bottom as everything in or around it sought shelter and hibernation from the bitter cold.

The boy stood on the edge of the marsh-pond, arms folded, chin out.

Azalea splashed him with the warm water.

3

"Come on, Oak-Lea, play the game," she said. "I'll give you a head-start."

Oak-Lea rolled his eyes. Then he took off his shoes with bad-tempered speed and plonked them down on a log. His mother had made them from lily-pad skin, so they were waterproof and buoyant like river-ducks, but they somehow pulled him down to the pond-bed like boulders.

The boy tested the water with his biggest toe before lowering himself into the pool, keeping hold of the bank with both hands the whole time.

"What we're looking for are those little bronze ones," said Azalea. "You know, with the grey tails? They're slippery and they're small, so make sure you seal up your fingers when you catch one," to which the boy nodded. "Don't squeeze them though," she added. "You'll hurt them."

Oak-Lea shivered despite the warmth of the water.

"We en't supposed to catch fish, Az. If your ma finds out—"

"Oak-Lea Moss, are you scared of my mother?"

"No," he replied, a little too quickly perhaps. "Course not."

Azalea disappeared under the water, slipping between the rocks of the pond's bed like a sea-snake and pulling at the hairs of her friend's feet as she went.

Oak-Lea wasn't like her, not when it came to fish-catching, not when it came to anything much. They were children of the Homotium species, so Azalea was already twice his size and not yet fully-grown. She swam like a mountain-salmon, her leaf-dress flowing impressively around her legs, sleek and undulating like fins, as if having grown from her body for that very purpose. Whereas Oak-Lea's clothes came to life in the water, resolute to throttle or drown him, or both.

Through the swarming pond-life the girl gazed up as his face broke the surface of the water. So many fish! Flash-barbs and pond-pike, white-tetras and long-eared catfish – Azalea knew them all at a glance. But Oak-Lea? He had no clue which eel was this or what shark was that, largely because naming fish was difficult when the front of your leaf-shirt kept floating in front of your face.

The boy lifted his head out of the water and peeled the duckweed from his neck as Azalea burst through the glittering shell of the pond with her hands cupped in the air.

"Did you even go under?" she frowned.

"No, this duckweed just leapt up and stuck itself to my face."

Azalea laughed.

"I told you, you gotta keep moving or you'll get

tangled. You're too slow, pal, that's your problem." She held out her hands, opening her thumbs to show him her catch. "He's tiny, isn't he? Do you reckon he's smaller than yesterlight's?"

"Yeah," smiled the boy, "I reckon he is."

She placed her catch carefully back in the water then they climbed from the marsh-pond to sit on the bank. The reddening sun settled on the Farnorthern Hills as a flock of spring-larks fell upon distant trees.

It was almost time to go home.

"I'd like to be a fish," said Azalea, drying her feet on a velveteen-fir leaf. "A fish can go anywhere it wants. Down wild rivers, up mountain streams, or across the ocean to visit the distant land. Just think, Oak-Lea, there could be all kinds of animals over there, and maybe another species like ours."

"Little green people live in the stars, Az, not on the distant land," he said, grimacing into the water, "and I can't think of anything worse than being a fish."

"Not even going into the mechanicary house?"

He tied his shoes at the back of his ankles.

"There en't nothing worse than going into the mechanicary hou—" He paused, remembering an earlier conversation. "Wait, we're not still going there at first lightness, are we?"

"Course. It's all arranged now."

"But the last time we went into the ruin you left me in there on my own."

"I did not. Ceanotha was with you."

"Yeah, and some comfort *she* was. That female's got a grip like a limpet-crab. Eight lightnesses later and I've still got the bruises to prove it."

Azalea laughed.

"Ceanotha Vine is a gazillion seasons old, Oak-Lea, she just *looks* a bit scary, that's all. Anyway, Bryony's meeting us there after sunrise and we can't back-out now. Imagine the smug look on her face if we don't turn up. We can't have Bryony Vine calling you a shadow-roach, can we?"

"I don't care what Bryony does. It's her grandmother I'm worried about."

"Ooh, scary old Ceanotha Vine," teased the girl. "Is there anyone's ma you en't scared of?" and squeezing the wet from her hair, she headed towards the grassway.

The Homotium people had walked to and from their village for so many seasons that a path had worn into the land. It started near the shingles of the Great Western Beach, snaked uphill past the lavender field and around the side of the restricted woodland, before heading east to the Homotium village.

The two friends dashed along it as the lightness

7

faded.

When they reached the roots of Azalea's tree, she leapt onto the trunk like a young wood-squirrel.

"I'll howl for you at first lightness then?" she said.

Oak-Lea wasn't sure if that was a question or not.

"Fine," he sighed, and she vanished into the leaves before he could change his mind. "But if you abandon me again, I'm telling your ma!" he called after her.

Azalea's tree was not the grandest in the village. Many homes in Midpoint Forest had wider trunks or more branches, and some had thicker bark with roots that bulged up like a female's bicep.

But to Azalea, hers was the best tree of all. It was straighter than most and taller too, and it seemed to be reaching for something beyond the forest. She didn't mind how out of place it looked. She didn't care that it was a pine-tree and the others were beech. All she cared about was how safe she felt in its branches, not to mention the fact she could see across the entire island from her sleeping-hut window. That tree was her kindred spirit and she wanted to live amongst its leaves forever.

Azalea scuttled to the top-most branch like a rain-beetle, just in time to see the crest of the blushing sun dip below the distant skyline. As darkness fell, a silvery glimmer of light washed over her eyes. Her vision grew suddenly clearer and she saw the world with bat-like clarity. She smiled as the light danced on the doorway in front of her.

Parting the lengths of dried grasses, Azalea hurried into the living-hut. A stone fire-pit burned at the centre of the room, above which hung the hollowed trunk of a sapling-oak through a hole in the ceiling. It served as a smoke funnel and allowed the fumes from the burning lavender to escape from the forest.

Azalea's mother sat close to the fire, stoking the snow-like flowers with a thick branch.

"Just because you've got your dark-vision now," she said, "doesn't mean it's safe to be out after sunfall." Marjoram Fern was not someone you could come home late to. Not happily, anyway. "Have you been fish-catching again?"

The glow from the fire hit Azalea's eyes and extinguished their light.

"I en't been nowhere near the marsh-pond. You told me to leave the fish alone, remember?"

Marjoram's gaze drifted across the room to Azalea's damp hair. She stoked the flames harder as she threw a handful of lavender into the fire.

"There's a plate of stewed leaves and toasted nuts on the side," she said, "and stop saying, en't, you know I don't like it."

Azalea pulled a face behind her mother's back for as long as she dared, then she fetched the bowl and sat on a laced-fungus mat.

"Thanks, Ma," she said, scooping the food hungrily into her mouth, "it's good. Have we got any melon juice?"

Marjoram put down her stick as if it was the last stick she would ever put down.

"Ceanotha Vine found Oak-Lea Moss in the mechanicary house a few lightnesses ago. Did you know about it?"

Azalea coughed and a pine nut shot out of her mouth.

"No. Do we have any melon juice or not?"

"He had a friend with him. One who ran off like a young antelope. Quick as a mountain-cat, according to Ceanotha."

Azalea felt her cheeks turn pink. She moved her mat closer to the fire so the heat would account for their redness.

"I'm not Oak-Lea's *only* friend," she said, "and anyway, I don't see what the big deal is. It's just a pile of old bricks."

Marjoram took a breath to contain her frustration, then began her next sentence as if starting a story of epic proportions.

"Many seasons ago," she said, "Iris Green went into the mechanicary house—"

"Oh, Ma, not the Iris Green story again!"

"*Iris Green went into the mechanicary house*," she repeated, this time with raised eyebrows, "and she caught the sickness from the bones of the extinct. Iris died three lightnesses later and Ceanotha Vine's son met the same fate not long after. Whatever caused the extinction of the Sapien people still lingers on the bones in that building, Azalea. Two people from our village have died because of it. I forbid you to die too."

"You forbid me to *die?*"

"For the time being, yes," snapped her mother. Her mask slipped and she sighed heavily. "Just promise you'll stay out of the ruin, Azalea. It's dangerous."

The girl shoved some more food into her mouth and nodded, and Marjoram turned back to the fire. But her mother's words had landed like snow, settling without impact and melting away into nothing. There was no way Azalea would let Bryony think she was scared of an old building. At first lightness she would prove her bravery by going into the ruin and if her mother didn't like it, she would just have to make sure she didn't find out.

CHAPTER 3
CAN WE JUST GET ON WITH THIS?

The sun rose to the rustle of movement on the forest ground. Some of the other villagers had just left the lavender harvest, their tired feet dragging as they walked home to their trees. During springtime, the flowers were white and at their most fragrant, so they had to be picked by moonlight or the buttermoths would smother you in the process. They flocked to the field in their millions, brightly-coloured paper-winged angels of the lightness, some as big as your head, some as small as your fingernail, warming the pale lavender like a patchwork blanket of life.

Azalea loved sitting amongst the stems, out of sight, watching the buttermoths dance on the buds near her head. Her mother compared it to waking one lightness and finding an enormous mountain-bear watching you sleep. But a bear would eat a Homotium, whereas Azalea only wanted to look at the buttermoths.

The girl had already got dressed and climbed up to

12

the living-hut when her father arrived home with a harvesting bag full of lavender.

"You're up early," he said. "The sun's not even out yet. Are you going somewhere?"

Aspen Fern was calm like the summer air. The lines of his whiskered face rarely showed anger or annoyance. He was a full head and shoulders shorter than his daughter, but they had the same eyes and they shared the same curiosity for the world around them.

"I'm meeting Oak-Lea at first lightness," she said, tying her leaf-dress at the back of her neck. "We're going, erm, buttermoth-catching." Azalea knew that pretending to be honest about something *small* she shouldn't be doing was the best way to hide something *big* she shouldn't be doing. "You won't tell Ma, will you?"

"You hold them, you look at them, you set them free," he replied with a smile. "The little ones like limes, so try those first, and if your mother finds out...I know nothing."

"Thanks, Pa," she said.

Oak-Lea's tree was on the southern side of Midpoint Forest, where he lived with his mother and five younger siblings. Their father died shortly after the birth of the quintuplets and the boy's mother joked that the shock of five babies was enough to kill anyone. But everyone knew she missed him sorely and covered his absence with laughter for the sake of her young family.

Azalea picked up a pine cone. She threw it at the small wooden hut on the lowest branch. It struck the wall with a dull thud and a window-shutter opened.

A freckled face appeared in the frame.

"When you said, first lightness, I didn't know you meant *literally* first lightness," hissed Oak-Lea. "And stop throwing stuff – you'll wake the boys up."

"Sorry," she said. "I'll howl instead," and she took a breath in fake preparation.

"No!" he cried. "Stay there and I'll come down."

He was carrying a small basket when he reached the roots of the tree. Between the woven threads, Azalea saw fruits and berries, and there, sticking out of the top, a handful of limes.

"I told Ma we're going buttermoth-catching," said the boy, "and she made a fruit salad for us to take. I feel bad for lying to her now."

"It en't our fault we have to lie," she said. "We need to stop Bryony looking down her snout at us. She reckons she's so much better than everyone else, just because her grandmother is Ceanotha Vine," and Oak-Lea shuddered at the sound of the old female's name.

As they walked through the forest, the air grew thick with the sounds and smells of the early lightness:

fresh dew on garlic shoots, the chatter-lark gossiping in the spring trees, the old cow-bull moaning from a nearby field and a southerly breeze carrying the scent of sea-water from the Crystal Shore. They made their way past the marsh-pond and through the knotted undergrowth, until they came to a rope of thorns on the ground.

This was the boundary that marked-out the restricted area. Ceanotha had placed it there many seasons ago and it was not to be crossed under any circumstance. But Azalea marched over it and Oak-Lea paused for no more than a heart-beat before running to catch up with her.

A sheet of mayweed lay strewn over the ground on the other side of the boundary, then a tall patch of sweet-nettles slowed their pace. They made their way under a blossoming cherry-bush and paddled through a narrow stream, until the old mechanicary house came into view.

The last Sapien ruin rested on the southernmost side of the restricted woodland like the remnant of a forgotten world. It dominated the landscape with eerie symmetry, vast and intimidating yet somehow fragile like snow. The other Sapien buildings had crumbled long ago, but the mechanicary house boasted four walls, a roof, three rows of barred windows and a line of symbols above the entrance.

Bryony Vine leaned against the brick wall, her white-blonde hair perched neatly on top of her head like a parakeet's crown, bejewelled with berries and held in place by a strand of poison-ivy.

Seeing Azalea, she placed both hands on her hips and pouted.

"Nice leaf dress," she smirked, smoothing her freshly waxed bark-sleeve. "It's very...*leafy*, isn't it? Aw, and you brought little Oak with you. How sweet."

"It's Oak-*Lea*," growled Azalea. "You know he took his father's name after he died. You're such a sludge-stirrer, Bryony."

The girl snorted.

"If *my* father had been stupid enough to go out during winter, I wouldn't want anything to do with his name."

"Don't talk about Oak-Lea's pa like that! You know he died rescuing the old cow-bull from the snow. Without him we'd have no cattle and no milk."

Bryony pushed a loose strand of hair away from her face.

"Let me get this right," she said. "*My* father died because he went into a plague-ridden ruin to investigate an ancient sickness, after which my grandmother laid a thorned boundary that protects our entire species, and *his* father died for a cow?"

She cackled like a kookaburra.

"I swear, if you don't shut your mouth, Bryony—"

"You'll *what?*" snarled the girl.

"Stop it, both of you!" Oak-Lea knew this conversation had nothing to do with his father, not really. "Can we just get on with this so I can go home please?"

"*You're* going in there too?" laughed Bryony. "Surely not. I've seen more backbone on a river-slug than on little *Oak* Moss."

Azalea stared the girl unblinkingly in the eye then turned to the wooden door of the ruin. Occasional green flakes clung to its weathered panels, some of which dropped to the ground as she reached out her hand and pushed.

"Come on, Oak-Lea," she said, as the door opened with a creak of complaint. "Let's go."

The shadows enveloped them like a mist. Azalea's dark-vision flickered alight, illuminating part of the room. The floor was slick with green like the algae-encased boulders of the Eastern Cliffs and rock-millipedes scuttled in and out of the cracks. The windows were blocked by creepers and a vine-encased ceiling hovered over them like an angry storm-cloud. To see the room in such detail made the Sapien world feel strangely tangible, like the unburst bubble of a lost season, and Azalea gazed around it with wonder until a crash came from the entrance.

A downpour of rubble fell from the rafters. When the deluge stopped, Azalea squinted through the dust-filled air and a sickening feeling swelled in her stomach – the mechanicary house door had been closed.

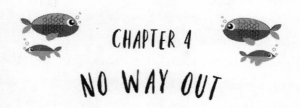

CHAPTER 4
NO WAY OUT

Azalea ran to the door and hammered her fists on the wood.

"Let us out!" she shouted. "This en't funny, Bryony!"

Oak-Lea paced the floor, his eyes large like chicken eggs.

"We've had it," he said. "We're goners. I knew we shouldn't have come here."

"Stop being such a pea-cock, Oak-Lea. There en't no bones in the top section of the ruin. Just try to calm down."

"Calm down? Az, she's locked us inside the *mechanicary house!* I don't even have my dark-vision yet. I have to get out," and he tipped back his head to howl.

"Don't!" cried Azalea. The boy stopped. "I'd rather take my chances with the Sapien sickness than with my ma. I won't be allowed out for the rest of the season if she finds out I'm in here." She pressed her ear to the door. "I reckon Bryony's gone. Let me see if I can get some light in here for you."

The room was in darkness except for the glow of Azalea's eyes and a dull smudge of sunlight seeping in from a corner of the room, where one of the windows was not quite fully blocked by creepers. Azalea ran to it. She rummaged amongst the leaves, found the thickest stem and pulled. It snapped audibly, so she tugged at another, and another, and soon the sunlight flowed more readily into the room.

"There," she said, her dark-vision fading. She eyed the barred window. "Can you fit between those?"

"Sure. If you slice me up like a vine-melon."

Azalea pulled a face.

"It's a shame we can't saw through the bars with your razor-sharp wit, isn't it? There must be another way out."

A hole in the back wall was partly hidden amongst a tangle of plants and arachni-bug webs. Azalea went over and dragged the foliage to one side. A flight of climbing-steps appeared, leading down into the darkness. The Homotium were familiar with these strange Sapien structures. There were some carved into the White Rocks of the Great Western Beach and more leading up the back of the Farnorthern Hills. As youngsters, Azalea and Oak-Lea would run up and down them like tree-bears, pretending they were the sole survivors of the Sapien extinction.

"Erm, what're you doing?" asked Oak-Lea.

"Getting us out of here," she said.

Azalea took hold of the rails on either side of the steps.

"No way," said the boy, "I'm not going down there. That's where the bones are."

"We can't just stand here doing nothing," she told him. "If we can't escape, we'll come straight back up again." She looked pleadingly at the boy. "I don't want to go on my own, Oak-Lea," and with a last look at the closed door, he nodded.

As they moved carefully down the stairwell, Azalea snapped the arachni-bug webs from their path. The ancient steps groaned under the weight of the children and the air grew thick with the smell of mould, until a soft light pressed up through the darkness.

Azalea quickened her pace, taking the climbing-steps three at a time, before coming to a halt at the bottom.

"What is it?" called Oak-Lea, catching up with her. "What can you see? There's no way out, is there."

Azalea stepped onto the green floor. Sunlight poured in from above her; she sensed it even though she did not look up. For there, like the discarded shell of a giant, prehistoric insect, lay the rusted Sapien mechanicary in heavy silence, tired and motionless in its forgotten grave.

Azalea walked towards it. She reached out her hand and stroked it like a sick animal. The dirt crumbled from its shell and she squinted with interest, realising she could see *through* this part of the casing. The mechanicary was hollow and its innards were lined with rows of raised seating.

"It's been burrowing," gaped Oak-Lea, leaving the stairwell. "Look."

He pointed to the outline of a warren-like tunnel in the side wall. The ceiling had collapsed and the fallen-earth was blocking the hole, but a row of arched bricks still marked the roof of the passageway.

"It en't been burrowing," she said. "My pa reckons the Sapiens built lots of these tunnels and the mechanicaries moved through them on an underground rail. Groups of their species would sit on those seats and ride around in them from place to place. They were pack animals, see, and dangerous too, I expect."

She brushed another section of mould from the mechanicary to reveal a small handle behind it. She squeezed her fingers into the hole and pulled.

Something clicked, then a large piece of the shell clattered onto the ground. The noise bounced around the chamber like rock-fall as a rancid smell spewed out from inside the mechanicary.

"The sickness," coughed Oak-Lea. "We have to go," and he made a dash for the stairwell.

"Wait!" Azalea covered her mouth with her arm, as Oak-Lea slid to a halt on the wet stone floor. "Look, up there. Those creepers are hanging down from the restricted woodland. If we get on top of the mechanicary, we could reach for one and climb out from the back of the ruin."

"What, you mean, like, *touch* it?"

"Yes, I mean, like, touch it," she said, "unless you have any better ideas."

"I dunno, Az…"

"What else are we meant to do? Sit up there and hope Bryony comes back for us. It's the only way, Oak-Lea. Come on, I'll lift you up."

Taking his hands, she hauled him onto her shoulders. He scrambled onto the top of the mechanicary and Azalea pulled herself up to join him.

The surface was damp, slippery and hard to stand on. Azalea reached for the nearest creeper and passed it to Oak-Lea. They had climbed these plants their whole lives and this one was no different, so they shimmied up it with speed before hauling themselves onto the ground of the woodland.

"Well, that could've been worse," Azalea eventually said, as they lay on the grass at the back of the ruin.

Oak-Lea's forehead creased.

"*How* exactly?"

"I mean, we didn't see any bones, so we probably won't catch the sickness."

"Oh, well, if we *probably* won't die, that's okay then."

Azalea sat up.

"Come on, worry-worm," she said, jumping to her feet before pulling Oak-Lea to his, "let's get out of here before Bryony tells the whole village where we are."

They followed the edge of the restricted woodland to the thorned rope on the easterly side of the trees. Here, the boundary ran alongside the grassway, where a group of Homotium were making their way towards the Great Western Beach. If Azalea was seen leaving the woodland, her mother would be furious, so they hid in a blue-hawthorn bush to wait for the coast to be clear.

Suddenly, two figures walked onto the grassway. They stopped near the plum-berry grove.

"It's *Bryony*," snarled Azalea, peering out from their hiding place. "She thinks we're still inside the mechanicary house and there she is smiling and laughing without a care in the world. She's such a wart-toad."

"Az, don't do nothing stupid," urged Oak-Lea. "There's no point in making it worse."

"I bet she's telling that girl from the Farnorthern Village what she did to us," Azalea went on. "Let's get closer so we can hear what she's saying," and before Oak-Lea could stop her, she was slithering towards the boundary like a bush-adder.

Bryony straightened her mass of billowing white hair and shifted her weight to one side.

"And then I just slammed the door," she said. "My grandmother wanted me to scare them away from the ruin for good and I doubt they'll want to set foot in there ever again after this. You know my grandmother, right? She's practically the village sage and she puts me in charge of all kinds of stuff."

"She's such a liar," growled Azalea. "Ceanotha wouldn't put Bryony in charge of a fruit-fly."

"Az, come on, let's just sneak out and go home."

"Shush, Oak-Lea. I can't hear what she's saying."

She wriggled closer to the grassway.

"Imagine little Oak Moss's face when he realised what I'd done," said Bryony. "Azalea will probably be all right, but *he* wouldn't survive a crane-gnat's bite, let alone the Sapien sickness. I mean, his father couldn't even survive the winter, for field's sake."

A flush of angry heat rose to Azalea's chest.

"Right," she seethed, "that's it!" and she swept from the woodland like a summer-typhoon, stopping no more than a breath away from the girl's face.

"For your information, Bryony," she spat, "Oak-Lea is fine. But you're about to wish you'd never been born."

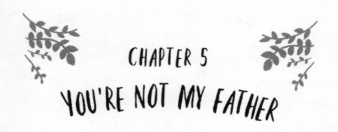

CHAPTER 5
YOU'RE NOT MY FATHER

"Oh good, you got out," grinned Bryony, her voice dripping with sarcasm. "I don't know how the door slammed closed like that."

Azalea longed to wipe the smirk from her face.

"You put our lives in danger just so you could show-off to your friend?" she said. The Farnorthern girl looked at her feet. "I can't believe you did that, Bryony."

"And *I* can't believe you just came out of the restricted woodland, Azalea. That's two out-of-bounds places in one lightness. What *will* Marjoram say?"

Azalea could feel the fury boiling inside her.

"At least I've *got* a mother," she retorted. "I reckon yours left 'cause she was sick of seeing your smug face."

There was silence, both girls deciding their next move, until Bryony's back arched like a field-leopard and she lashed out with her fingernails. They caught the side of Azalea's neck, as a voice cried out from behind them.

"Hey! What's going on over there?" Bryony's brother stormed towards them along the grassway, his white face-hair knotted in tiny loops on his temples and his crystal-white eyes reflecting the spring sunlight. He peered at the scratch on Azalea's neck. "Did you do this to her?"

"She was asking for it," muttered Bryony.

"And you did *nothing*, I suppose?" said Azalea.

Rowan Vine glowered at his sister.

"If you have a problem with someone, Bryony, sort it out without the use of your fingernails." He tipped his head towards the plum-berry grove. A female harvester from the Farnorthern Village was watching them through her thick hair. "People are looking at us. You shouldn't be dirtying the name of our family by fighting like a bear."

Bryony's face pulled taut.

"You can't tell me what to do, Rowan. You're not my father."

The boy's cheeks reddened.

"You are unbelievable," he said. "Just come home before I tell Grandmother what you've done," and without waiting for a reply, he walked towards the village.

28

Bryony hesitated before following after him, leaving the Farnorthern girl with Azalea and Oak-Lea. She scuffed her foot in the dirt, flashed an apologetic smile at the pair of them, and then scuttled away like a log-louse.

"Ugh!" cried Azalea. She thundered along the grassway in the opposite direction. "Bryony Vine is so *annoying!*"

Oak-Lea said nothing. He simply watched her walk to the lavender field, a flood of buttermoths rising up as she entered the flowers. She lay on her back and stretched her hands up into the buds, the wings of the insects and the smell of the lavender gradually calming her temper.

Oak-Lea picked his way through to join her.

"Shall we try to catch a miniature-fireflash?" he suggested. "I left the fruit basket back at the mechanicary house, but I reckon we could try without it."

"All right," She paused, and then, "I shouldn't have said that," she added. "About her ma, I mean."

"You were angry, and Bryony's said worse to us."

"Yeah, but imagine not knowing if your own mother is dead or alive. My pa said it was as if someone had snatched her away in the darkness. One moment she was there, and the next she wasn't."

"Primrose Vine was sick," he said. "My ma reckons she probably took herself off to die so her children didn't have to watch. Bryony was really young when she left. She probably don't even remember her."

Azalea felt miserable. She had never got along with Bryony, but she knew better than to twist the knife about something like that. The girl's father had died a few seasons after her mother went missing and she'd been raised by her grandmother ever since. Azalea knew it was cruel to have mentioned it, even in the heat of the moment.

"I still reckon she's a wart-toad though," she huffed. *"Look at me, Bryony Vine, guardian of the mechanicary house, the most important Homotium in the village.* I've seen fruit-parrots less cocky. There's no way Ceanotha has put her in charge of anything."

A crested-owlwing settled on Oak-Lea's finger. The boy flinched and then glanced at Azalea in the hope she hadn't noticed, which she had.

"You know who probably *did* tell Bryony to trap us in the mechanicary house though?" said the girl.

"No. Who?"

"The *buttermoths!*"

"Ha ha," he said, flatly. "I en't scared of them, Az."

"Course not," she grinned. A tiny buttermoth with a fiery splash of orange on each of its wings alighted on the tip of her finger. She held it out to show him and the insect fluttered away. "Do you want to get something to eat? My ma will make us something if you come back to my tree. Last one there's a rotten fungus!"

At mid-lightness, the village buzzed with life. Young Homotium played in the shade of the trees, fully-growns foraged for nuts and the elderly folk whittled stories of the past into the trunks of unoccupied trees. There was so much to look at that neither Azalea nor Oak-Lea noticed Marjoram until they were almost on top of her.

She was standing at the foot of her tree with a face like a tree-baboon without a banana. Azalea knew the look well. It meant the girl had done something wrong, something her mother didn't want the neighbours to find out about. It was the face of someone happily suffering a terrible pain and it could only mean one thing – *she knew they'd been in the mechanicary house!*

Marjoram's smile turned into a grimace as the children approached the tree.

"Get - up - those - branches," she said, through gritted teeth, "before - I - properly - lose - my - acorns." She leaned in and lowered her voice. "Ceanotha Vine is in our living-hut. She knows where you were at first lightness, so get up those branches and explain yourselves to her right now. And Azalea, whatever that is on your neck, *do not* mention it in front of her."

Marjoram leapt into the branches, as Oak-Lea's face started to sweat.

"What're we going to say?" he panicked. "What're we going to tell them?"

"We're going to tell them the truth," said Azalea. "We're going to tell them that Bryony Vine is a nasty swamp-rat who likes trapping people inside the mechanicary house. It's about time Ceanotha Vine knew what her precious granddaughter is *really* like."

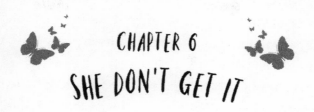

CHAPTER 6
SHE DON'T GET IT

Ceanotha Vine's floor-length white hair rested on her shoulders in a thick braid. It curled like a snow-python, framing the deep lines of her face with ethereal radiance, the light of the lavender illuminating its pallor so her skin appeared bark-like and worn. She was holding a staff of maple-wood in one hand and the root of a plant in the other.

Azalea burst through the grass doorway like a field-rhino through a poppy field.

"It was Bryony's fault," she said, before the old female could speak. "She lured us into the mechanicary house, then she slammed the door and blamed the whole thing on you. Oh, and then she did *this* with her scabby nails. Look."

Marjoram's face trembled like a ripe seed-pod, as Azalea tilted her head to show Ceanotha the wound.

"I'm sure Bryony's not to blame," her mother babbled, like a fresh-water stream. "Azalea probably said something to provoke her. What did she say to her, Oak-Lea?"

The boy jumped as if having been slapped with a large sea-cod.

"Well, I mean, Azalea says all sorts of things." He wasn't sure if telling the truth extended to what had been said about Bryony's mother. "It's hard to remember them all, but I think she probably said something about Bryony's..." Azalea's eyes bulged like pebbles. "...erm, hair," he finished, uncertainly.

"As if!" snorted Azalea. "Why would I care about Bryony Vine's hair? Anyway, whatever I said was *after* she trapped us inside the ruin."

Ceanotha held the cream-coloured plant root close to the fire and turned it in the heat of the flames.

"Bryony can be challenging," she said, "but the wound on your neck will heal. The Sapien sickness, however, will not."

"We en't sick," said Azalea. Marjoram winced at the middle word of that sentence. "There's nothing wrong with us."

"If you're infected," the old female replied, "your symptoms won't show right away. But we have to prepare for the worst and this plant root can stop the sickness spreading into your bones."

She broke the warmed root in half. She handed one

34

piece to Oak-Lea and the other to Azalea. Its insides were fibrous and grey, and there was a brown streak running through the middle of it like a vein.

"I eat this when I'm feeling unwell," said the old female, "but there are no guarantees it will work. By the time Iris Green ate the root, the Sapien sickness had already got into her bones, and my dear Thornton was beyond help as well."

"That's comforting," Azalea muttered.

Marjoram threw her a look, as Ceanotha stared quietly at the floor.

"But you are both young and strong," she said, lifting her gaze, "so I am hopeful I've got to you fast enough."

"Hm," said Azalea, eyeing the awful-looking plant, "but we didn't see any bones, so we'll probably be fine without it."

"Oh, well, if you *probably* won't die, that's okay then," snapped Marjoram.

"That's what *I* said," added Oak-Lea.

Ceanotha pulled back her thin shoulders.

"The Sapien bones were buried when the ground above them collapsed," she told them, "but the sickness is nevertheless strong in the lower section. I assume you exited the building through the underground chamber?" Azalea gave a guilty nod.

"Did you touch anything while you were down there?"

"No," she lied. Ceanotha eyed her algae-stained clothes. "I mean, we had to touch some of the creepers to climb out, but we didn't go near the mechanicary."

Azalea brought the gruesome-looking plant root to her mouth before the old female could ask any more questions. It smelt bitter like unripe lemon-plums yet somehow sweet like cow-butter. It reminded her of a vomit-fruit she had been tricked into eating by one of Oak-Lea's brothers.

Azalea fixed her eyes on the ceiling and shoved it into her mouth. The boy did the same.

"The first one always tastes worse than the others," said Ceanotha, heading towards the door.

"The others?" scowled Azalea, still chewing. "What others?"

"You'll need a second dose," the female explained, "maybe even a third. Marjoram, bring them to my tree shortly after sun rise and I'll have it ready for them," and parting the grass with her stick, the old female left the tree.

Oak-Lea followed soon after, keen to escape the narrow-eyed glare of Azalea's mother. But Azalea was forbidden to leave the tree for the next few lightnesses and was given a long list of chores as punishment for her behaviour: bundling the lavender, shelling horse-

36

chestnuts, thickening the cow-milk and peeling enough fruit to feed a family of cave-bats for the whole of winter.

The endless sky called to her through the slats of her living-hut ceiling. She watched it stretch out over the forest, morphing from blue to pink to pebble-grey, until darkness swamped the village like the tide stealing over the Crystal Shore.

"I want you to help your father at the lavender harvest during darkness," said Marjoram.

Aspen offered Azalea a plate of boiled pea-shoots as if offering his condolences.

"Can't I harvest when the sun's out?" asked the girl.

"It's a punishment, Azalea, not an outing. I don't want you leaving your father's side for so much as a heartbeat."

"Not even if I need the sewage hole?"

"Not even if you burst into flames and require the sewage hole to put yourself out," replied Marjoram. "There'll be no wandering off, no daydreaming and no going near the restricted area. If I find out you've done any of those things, you won't leave this tree for the rest of the season." She threw a freshly woven tea-towel in her daughter's direction. "You can help with the washing-up before you go."

When the eating-bowls had been cleaned and dried,

Azalea placed the last of them into the basket and left the tree with her father. He hadn't said much that lightness, but as they sauntered through the velvety air of Midpoint Forest, he whispered, "And no breathing. Absolutely no breathing for the rest of your life or you won't leave this tree again for a gazzilion seasons."

Azalea laughed and took hold of his hand, their dark-vision dancing over the ground as they walked along the grassway.

"Have you ever been in the mechanicary house, Pa?" she asked, as they stopped to stroke the old cow-bull's nose.

"No, Azzy. The ruins have always been dangerous. Not because of the sickness, we didn't know about that until Iris Green died, but because they were ancient and likely to fall down. In fact they *did* all fall down apart from the mechanicary house. That's another reason you should stay out of there."

The old cow-bull rubbed its head on her father's shoulder.

"I know, Pa," she said, "but it's so creepy in there. The inside of the building is covered in vines and the underground section looks like it used to be part of a tunnel."

"Azzy, I can't condone what you did by talking about it with you."

"Before the woodland ground collapsed and blocked the entrance to the passageway," she went on, regardless, "the mechanicary house tunnel must've gone right underneath the restricted woodland. And you should see the mechanicary, Pa. You know the one on the eastern side of the Farnorthern Hills?"

Aspen tried not to look at her.

"Yes," he said.

"It's similar to that only ten times bigger and its windows are solid but you can see *through* them."

Her father stopped stroking the old cow-bull.

"What, like ice?"

"Yeah, but clearer and warmer and perfectly smooth…"

Azalea continued her story as they followed the grassway west and rounded the bend on the northern side of the woodland. A field of white blazed through the darkness, brightening the land like snowfall.

The other lavender harvesters had already arrived. Azalea and her father joined them, working in silence until the moon slid to the other side of the sky, at which point they packed up their tools and carried their lavender back to the village.

Azalea stretched out her arms as she watched them leave.

"I'm exhausted," she yawned. "How do you do this

39

all the time, Pa?"

"We sometimes finish later than this," he said, absentmindedly. "Or earlier, depending on how you look at it."

He was staring across the field, his dark-vision lighting the northern side of the restricted woodland, seemingly lost in his own thoughts.

"That tunnel you were telling me about," he said, "do you really think it goes underneath the trees?"

"I reckon so. I suppose that's why Ceanotha restricted the woodland as well as the mechanicary house."

Aspen heaved a bag of lavender onto his shoulder as they left the field.

"Remember that elder-berry bush I found last autumn, Azzy?"

"I remember you finding berries," she said. "But I've never seen an elder bush this side of the Farnorthern Hills. Whereabouts is it?"

"Near the restricted woodland." He paused. "Well, I say *near*. It's more *in* it really."

Azalea gasped.

"Pa! You went into the restricted woodland for berries?"

"I know, I know, it was stupid of me. But we used to go into the woodland all the time when we were children, everyone did, so I just thought... I don't know what I thought. You know what I'm like. But since we spoke earlier, I've been thinking, and it's strange how I hadn't seen it before."

"I don't suppose you would've taken much notice of an elder bush when you were a child, Pa."

"No, I don't mean the bush. The bush has always been there." His face was pale in the light of her vision. "When I was looking for the elder-berries, I saw a doorway, a hatch in the ground, hidden underneath some fallen ivy. It must be an entrance to the other end of that tunnel you were telling me about."

"A doorway? Did you—"

"No," he replied, predicting the rest of her question. "You'd have to be crazy to open a doorway in the restricted woodland. The only reason I'm telling you this is because I want you to know I understand. You're curious and I get it. But nothing is more important than keeping yourself safe."

Azalea nodded.

"I just wish Ma felt the same. She don't get it at all."

"Oh, your mother understands more than you think. Marjoram Fern was as curious as a sand-fox when we were young and she still is deep down. But she's a mother now too, Azzy, and she worries about you. She wants to set a good example and so do I.

Which is why *I* won't go looking for that doorway again and *you* won't go in the mechanicary house. Deal?"

"Deal," smiled Azalea, and with a last look at the restricted woodland, they headed back to the village.

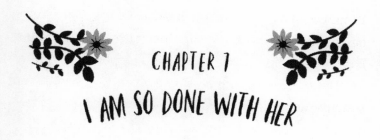

CHAPTER 7
I AM SO DONE WITH HER

"I've called you three times," said Azalea's mother. "Can you *please* get out of bed and get dressed? We've got to fetch Oak-Lea on the way to Ceanotha's."

Azalea sat up, eyes closed, brain fuzzy. She had literally *just* gone to sleep. The girl muttered something under her breath, words she wouldn't dare say if her mother was still in the room, then she got dressed and climbed down from the tree.

When they reached the trunk of Oak-Lea's home, Marjoram looked up at the neighbouring branches. A pointed nose poked out through a gap in the window-shutter.

"Don't say anything about going into the you-know-what," she whispered. "Flora Elm will take great pleasure in telling the whole village about your antics if she finds out. Just act like everything's normal."

"Everything *is* normal," Azalea replied.

Her mother howled into the branches and a tiny boy

dropped from the leaves. He fell towards Marjoram's head, stopping no more than a breath away from her face, where he swung from the creeper like a giant arachni-bug, flapping his arms and chewing on something black.

"What in the name of sunlight is *that?*" cried Marjoram.

"It's Oak-Lea's brother," Azalea said, tiredly. "I en't sure which one though."

"Not the *boy*. The thing in his mouth."

"Oh." Azalea squinted up at the offending object. "Looks like a water-slug."

"SYCAMORE-LEA!" The voice came like a clap of thunder. It shook the forest like an earth-tremor. "'OW MANY TIMES I GOTTA TELL YOU, DO *NOT* ANSWER THAT TRUNK ON YOUR OWN!"

It seemed the boy could not hear the voice, which was more than could be said for the rest of the forest. Instead of getting back on his branch, he turned upside-down and allowed the something black to drop from his mouth.

The slug landed on Marjoram's shoulder as Oak-Lea's face appeared through the leaves. He seized Sycamore-Lea by the ankle and the boy spun like a falling seed, kicking and growling and clutching the vine with his brown set of teeth, before disappearing

44

into the branches.

Flora Elm's shutter clattered open as the rest of her face joined her nose.

"Fields save us," muttered Marjoram, flicking the chewed mollusc from her dress. "What sort of a Homotium eats slugs?"

"That's a bit unfair," said Azalea. "He didn't eat it, he spat it out."

Her mother inspected the remains on her shoulder.

"Not *all* of it," she noted.

The leaves moved for a third time and a stick-like pair of legs sprung from the foliage. Then a tiny leaf-dress appeared and Marjoram covered Azalea's eyes to shield them from what was to follow.

"Rosa-Lea!" cried Marjoram, putting on a posh voice for the sake of Flora Elm's nose. "There are plenty of leaves in this forest – could you not find a few more to make that dress out of?"

A pair of muddied feet hit the ground, where the dress was pulled down to a more respectable level.

"Sorry, Marj," grinned the female, "you knows I en't never been good at clothes-making. Remember that outfit I made for our Oaks when he were a newborn? Fitted 'im like a cocoon on a maggot," and she howled with laughter at the memory.

Rosa-Lea Moss was as grounded as the land itself.

Someone found her under a white-rose bush as a baby and she was raised by an old childless couple in the Farnorthern Village. Some said she must've grown in the leaf-cabbage patch, some said the sky-storks had put her there, and some said no self-respecting vegetable or bird could be responsible for Rosa-Lea Moss.

"Your child spat at me," said Marjoram, pointing to the bits on her shoulder.

Rosa-Lea eyed the mess as Oak-Lea joined them at the roots of the tree.

"Our Sycamore-Lea don't 'alf eat some weird stuff," she said. "But *the body wants what the body needs*, that's what my Lea used to say. I dunno what kinda body needs slugs though. Do you like my new 'air cut?"

"You look like you've had an accident," said Marjoram.

"Short's the new long, Marj. It keeps the 'ead-lice away and you can weave a new tablecloth with the bits you cut off." Azalea's mother looked as if she might vomit. "What about these two and their shenanigans then, eh? I dunno where our Oak-Lea gets it from."

"I could hazard a guess," muttered Marjoram.

"You're a li'tle rascal, Oak-Lea Moss, en't you?" She took hold of her son by the cheeks and shook his head like a coconut. "A proper scamp, that's what you—"

She stopped, pulling his face towards her. "Well, I'll be ploughed," she breathed. "OUR OAKS IS GETTIN' 'IS FACE-HAIR! LOOK, MARJ, HE'S AS PRICKLY AS A GRASS-HOG'S BUM!"

"Rosa-Lea," uttered Marjoram, "keep your voice down. Not everyone wants to know about your son's face-hair."

"BUT IT'S CREEPIN' UP 'IS CHIN LIKE A BAD CASE OF SWAMP-FUNGUS!" Rosa-Lea nudged Azalea hard in the ribs. "Bet you'd already noticed it, Azzy, eh, right, eh?"

"Azalea's noticed nothing of the sort!" crowed Marjoram, forgetting herself before glancing up at Flora Elm's nose.

Rosa-Lea followed the line of her gaze.

"Oh, Marj," she said, "you en't bothered about what *she* thinks, are you?" She cupped her hands to her mouth. "THAT NOSEY OLD MARE WANTS TO MIND 'ER OWN BUSINESS, THAT'S WHAT *SHE* WANTS TO DO!"

"For field's sake, Rosa-Lea…"

"I dunno when you got so bothered about what other folk think, Marj. Remember when we were kiddies and Cherry Redwood dared us to go into that Sapien ruin up on the Farnorthern Hills? Primrose told your pa what we'd done and you squawked at 'er like

47

a tree-parrot."

Azalea's eyebrows dropped.

"*You* went into a Sapien ruin?"

"It was different back then," said Marjoram. "We didn't know about the sickness."

"But that ruin collapsed before I was born," said the girl, "so it was still dangerous. Rosa-Lea, what else did my mother get up to when she was my age?"

An enormous grin spread across Rosa-Lea's face.

"Well," she began, "there were this big fire-ants' nest up near the red-poppy field and one lightness your mother decided to put her foot in the 'ole and you'll never guess what 'appened—"

"Enough chattering," said Marjoram. "Ceanotha will be waiting for us. Come along, you two," and she hurried away to the sound of Rosa-Lea's laughter.

The Vine family lived on the eastern side of the forest. The trunk of their home was wider than most and intricate drawings had been carved into the bark. The pictures told a story of two seeds from the same flower that dispersed in opposite directions. One fell on dusty ground and the other fell on wet soil. Their roots were the same but each grew into a different flower, shaped by the land upon which it had grown. Ceanotha said it symbolised the ever-changing pathway of life, but Azalea just found it pretty to look at.

Marjoram howled their arrival and Ceanotha called for the three of them to ascend. Rowan was warming the plant root on the fire and the old female was watching over him from her chair.

"We really are grateful for your help, Ceanotha," began Marjoram, in her most well-to-do voice. "I don't know what Azalea was thinking, going into that ruin. She's very easily influenced, I'm afraid."

Rowan tore the root in two. He gave one piece to Azalea and the other to Oak-Lea.

"I en't *influenced* by Oak-Lea Moss," Azalea retorted.

"Really?" said her mother, from behind a fixed grin. "Then why do you make such bad choices?"

Azalea smiled back at her.

"Because it's hard to make *good* choices when your mother literally doesn't let you do anything. *Don't look at the fish, Azalea. Don't say en't, Azalea. Don't touch the buttermoths, Azalea. Don't go for a wee in the sewage hole, Azalea.*"

"That's not what I said and you know it," snapped Marjoram. "Stop being ridiculous."

"Wow, Ma, was that something else I'm not allowed to do?"

Her mother took a long, steadying breath.

49

"Before you eat that," she said, her voice calm despite the fire in her eyes, "I want you to apologise to Ceanotha. You shouldn't have blamed your poor decision-making on her granddaughter. Disrespecting the memory of the poor girl's father was bad enough, but pointing the finger of blame at her too is nothing short of a disgrace."

Resentment grew fast in the pit of Azalea's stomach.

"Bryony trapped me in the mechanicary house. It's *her* who should be sorry, not *me*. I en't going to apologise when I've done nothing wrong."

"Oh, Azalea," sighed Marjoram, "why can't you just do as you're told for once?"

"*And why can't you just be on my side for once?!*" shouted the girl.

The hut fell silent. Azalea's throat tightened. She blinked and a flow of heavy tears dropped down her face.

"There's no need to cry about it," muttered Marjoram.

The weight of their eyes sat heavy on Azalea's shoulders. She squeezed the root in her furious fist and then dashed out of the living-hut to the sound of her mother apologising for her outburst.

Fury poured down her cheeks as she raced through the forest, over the sand-dunes near the Crystal Shore, across the milking-cow field and onto the Great Western Beach. At the water's edge, she threw herself onto a flat boulder, heaving long, heated breaths into her lungs until the tears stopped falling. She wanted to stay there forever, or at least until darkness, until finally, as the sun reached the highest point in the sky, a voice sounded behind her.

"You all right?"

Azalea lifted her head.

"How long have you been there?"

"A while." Oak-Lea sat down on the rock. "But you looked like you wanted to be alone, so I waited."

"Sorry for saying I en't influenced by you," she told him. She laughed a little. "I mean, I *en't* influenced by you, but...you know."

"I know," he smiled.

"I don't understand why she's always like that, why she always puts on a face for the neighbours. Why can't she just be herself for once?"

"It could be worse," he said. "She could be so completely herself that she tells the whole village about your face-hair."

"Fair point," said the girl.

Oak-Lea signalled to her clenched fist.

"You haven't eaten yours yet then." Azalea uncurled her fingers to find the plant root still suffering her anger inside. She had forgotten it was there. "Your ma said I had to eat mine then and there, otherwise I would've waited for you and we could've done it together."

"So now she's telling *you* what to do as well? Unbelievable." Azalea looked down at her hand. "I am so *done* with her," and raising her fist in the air, she launched the plant root across the ocean.

It floated on top of the foaming water for a brief moment, before sinking into the waves.

"Az," gaped the boy, still staring out at the ocean, "I don't reckon you should've done that. You could get sick."

Azalea's eyes thinned.

"The only thing I'm sick of," she said, "is my mother."

CHAPTER 8
SO BE IT

They stayed on the beach for the rest of that lightness, the warm sand sliding between their toes as they walked towards the White Rocks. They splashed in stone-pools, collected shells and paddled through the shallow waves, until the red sun bled into a fading sky.

Azalea spotted a figure in the distance. Bryony was collecting sea-weed along the waterline.

"Oh, no," breathed Oak-Lea. "Az, please don't—"

"Hey!" Bryony turned as Azalea surged towards her. "Why did you tell your grandmother about the mechanicary house? My ma's gone volcanic."

"I do enjoy being shouted at for no good reason," said the girl, "really I do, but I didn't tell her anything. My grandmother was worried you'd catch the sickness, because you're not clever enough to stay out of places that could *literally kill you*, so she asked me to scare you away from the mechanicary house for good."

"You're lying," snarled Azalea. "Ceanotha wouldn't tell you to do that."

"She didn't think you'd be stupid enough to go into the underground chamber though," continued the girl, "let alone climb on the mechanicary. If you had just stayed where I left you, I would've come back and let you out. But now you've probably caught the sickness, so if you could go and breathe near someone else, Azalea, that would be great."

"Take responsibility for what you did, Bryony! There's no way your grandmother would put us in danger like that, so—" She paused. "Wait, how do you know we climbed on the mechanicary?"

Bryony breathed a sigh of impatience.

"My grandmother told me every word you said to her when she visited you yesterlight." The girl knitted her eyebrows. "And my nails are *not* scabby."

"Ceanotha didn't tell you. I lied when she asked me about it. Were you watching us?"

The girl snorted with laughter.

"Yes, Azalea, that's right. I risked my life wandering around the restricted area to watch you and Oak-Lea climb out of a hole." She flicked her hair over her shoulder. "Anyway, this was nice, but I'd rather be pulling out my own toenails than standing here talking to you. Don't go climbing out of any holes without me,

Azalea – I wouldn't want to miss the excitement," and she strutted away from the shore.

Azalea kicked at the shallow waves.

"She's so *irritating!*"

"Just ignore her," said Oak-Lea. "She only says things to get a reaction out of you."

"You know what I reckon? I reckon she shut us in there then ran round to the other side of the building so she could laugh at us. I bet that weird Farnorthern girl was with her too."

Azalea looked out at the endless ocean. The blazing sun had almost extinguished itself in the water and the light was dying fast.

"It's getting dark," she said, gloomily. "We'd better go. I suppose I'll have to face my ma at some point," but as she turned towards the shingles, a movement near the grassway caught her eye. She snatched hold of the boy's wrist. "Keep still," she whispered. "Don't move."

A female mud-lizard padded across the shingles. A yellow tooth hung lazily over her bottom lip and a deep scar marked the spot where her left eye had once been. She watched them carefully as she slid down the pebbled ground and onto the sand.

"Should we run?" breathed Oak-Lea, his voice barely audible.

"I don't think so," she told him. "Not yet." The mud-lizard stopped. She whipped her heavy tail across the ground, tipped back her head and roared. "*NOW!*" cried Azalea.

Keeping hold of Oak-Lea's wrist the whole time, she darted full-pelt up the shingles, dragging him to the top of the slope, onto the grassway and around the corner of the restricted woodland, where they finally doubled in two, gasping for air.

"That...was...close," panted Oak-Lea.

"Too close," Azalea agreed. She flashed a mischievous grin at the boy. "Saved your life though, didn't I," she teased.

"Where the heck have you two been?" The voice startled them. Azalea's father ran over from the other end of the grassway. "Your mother's really worried, Azzy. Didn't either of you notice how dark it was getting? And please tell me you didn't just come from the beach of all places?"

Before they could answer, a light appeared in the distance. It bounced along the grassway like a field-cricket.

Without warning, Aspen pushed them behind the trunk of an elm tree.

"What's going on?" asked Azalea. "Who are we hiding from?"

56

"No idea," whispered her father. "But if Marjoram finds out you've just left the beach, I'll never hear the end of it. Keep your dark-vision covered, Azzy, and I'll tell her I found you both in the village."

As the light drew closer, they realised it was coming from two pairs of eyes. Ceanotha and Rowan Vine were walking along the grassway. They paused at the side of the restricted woodland, scanned the area and then disappeared into the trees.

Oak-Lea's jaw practically fell off.

"Why are they going into the restricted area?" he asked.

"I dunno," Azalea replied, straining her neck to see which way they were going, "but I bet it's got something to do with that doorway."

"What doorway?"

"You might be right, Azzy," mused Aspen. "It's strange how they're creeping around in the darkness though. It's like they don't want anyone to see where they're going."

She looked at her father through wide eyes.

"Do you think they're okay, Pa? I mean, perhaps we should follow them. You know, just to make sure."

Oak-Lea snorted a tiny laugh.

"Good one, Az," he chuckled.

"It might be best to check on them," said Aspen. "If

we keep our distance, they won't know we're there."

"And the mud-lizards rarely come inland," Azalea added.

"Sorry," said Oak-Lea, a hint of laughter still in his voice, "but you two en't serious, are you?"

Aspen looked into the trees, then back at his daughter.

"All right," he decided, "let's do it. But stay close and don't tell your mother. That goes for you too, Oak-Lea," and the two of them stepped over the boundary and into the trees.

"Hey, you can't leave me out here on my own!" cried the boy.

"Keep your voice down," Azalea retorted. "We're not leaving you. Now, keep up in case we meet any more mud-lizards."

They picked their way through the undergrowth at speed, their feet catching on the twisted plants and brambles of the woodland ground.

"I thought one of you was bad enough," muttered Oak-Lea, trudging miserably behind them, "but now there are two of you it's like an actual living darkmare."

They followed Ceanotha and Rowan to a small clearing in the middle of the woodland, where they stopped. The two of them stood there in silence, as if waiting for something to happen. Aspen shielded his dark-vision and beckoned Azalea and Oak-Lea into a sweet-coriander bush. They watched through parted leaves as a third pair of eyes came out of the darkness.

"Did you speak to Parvan about what happened?" Ceanotha said to the stranger.

Azalea didn't recognise his face. He was a similar age to her father and dressed in peculiar clothing made out of a woven material.

"Yes," he replied. "She says if the two of them went into the mechanicary house once, they'll go in there again." Aspen silently shook his head in response to the look on Azalea's face. "She agrees we should build a boundary-fence and she asks that you do it as soon as possible."

"The extra security will do no harm," the old female replied, "but I've already secured the area in my own way."

The stranger froze.

"What do you mean, *in your own way?* What've you done?"

He turned his eyes to Rowan. But the boy looked at the ground.

"I asked Bryony to encourage them back into the mechanicary house," Ceanotha admitted, "and trap them inside. I knew their only way out would be through the underground section, so…"

She let that sentence hang in the air. The stranger's face turned grey.

"Not again," he breathed, shaking his head. "Please tell me you haven't done it again."

Ceanotha dug the end of her walking-stick into the soft ground and looked at him with stony eyes.

"If a few lives must be sacrificed for the good of our people," she said, "then so be it. I had no other choice."

"There is *always* a choice," the stranger snapped. "Putting up a new boundary-fence, *that* was the choice. Why couldn't you just wait until—"

"*Do not question me!*" Azalea had never heard Ceanotha raise her voice before. It made the skin on the back of her neck prickle. "If the other Homotium find out we've been lying to them, the trust we've built with Parvan will be ruined. Is that what you want, for all this to have been for nothing?"

"Of course not," he said.

"Then leave the protection of the ruin to me and concentrate on your own role." She replaced a loose strand of hair back behind her ear. "Does Parvan know when they will arrive?"

"Preparations are almost ready," he told her. "It won't be long. Let's meet in two lightnesses and I should know more by then," and nodding goodbye, the stranger went back into the darkness.

Ceanotha and Rowan left the woodland in silence. Azalea waited until they were gone before bursting out from the coriander bush.

"Oh, my fields!" she cried, hardly able to say the words fast enough. "Bryony was telling the truth. Ceanotha really *did* ask her to shut us inside the mechanicary house. Why would she put us in danger like that?"

Her father stared hard at the empty clearing.

"If a few lives must be sacrificed for the good of our people, then so be it," breathed Oak-Lea. "That's what she said. It sounded like she *wanted* us to get sick, Az."

"But why would she forage a cure for us if that's what she wanted? It don't make no sense."

Azalea studied her father. His eyes were still fixed on the place where the Vines had once stood.

"You don't remember him, do you?" he asked.

"The stranger?" she said. "I assumed he was from the Farnorth."

"No, he's from Midpoint Forest. You must've been too young when he…" Her father couldn't seem to find the end of that sentence. "That person we just saw talking to Ceanotha Vine, is her son."

Azalea looked at Oak-Lea then turned back to her father.

"Ceanotha's son is dead, Pa. The darkness must've been playing tricks on you."

"I wish it was, Azzy," replied Aspen, "but there's no doubt about it. Thornton Vine was here in this woodland, and he didn't look very dead from where I was standing."

CHAPTER 9
HE JUST LIES THERE

"Did you sleep well?" asked Aspen, preparing the breakfast oats.

"Not really," Azalea replied. "I couldn't stop thinking about it. Why would Ceanotha pretend her son was dead?"

"I don't know, and until we *do* know I want you and Oak-Lea to stay away from the Vines. And let's not worry your mother with any of this just yet either, okay?"

Marjoram blew in through the grass door like a winter breeze.

"What are you not going to worry me with?"

Aspen searched the ceiling for an answer, as if hunting for snowflakes in summer.

"We were just... The thing is... What happened was..."

"I went fish-catching yesterlight," said Azalea. "That's where I went after I ran out of Ceanotha's living-hut. Wow, it's a relief to get that off my chest," she added for good measure.

"Oh, Azalea," sighed her mother, "how many times do I have to—"

A howl sounded from the roots of the tree. It wasn't a howl of arrival, it was one of urgency, one that sent all three of them scrambling down the trunk, where Rosa-Lea was pacing the ground like a wounded tree-bear.

"Whatever's wrong?" asked Marjoram.

"It's our Oaks. He's proper poorly, Marj. He can't stand up and 'is face is all grey."

Azalea's heart banged like a drum.

"Aspen," said Marjoram, "you and Azalea take Rosa-Lea to her tree and make sure the boy drinks plenty of water. I'll howl for Ceanotha and meet you there," and she darted through the forest at speed.

At the foot of Oak-Lea's tree, five wide-eyed children were waiting. Aspen instructed them to stay where they were then he followed Rosa-Lea to the topmost branch with Azalea close behind him.

The fire had grown dim in the living-hut. Oak-Lea lay close to its embers, a knotted grass blanket covering his legs, his arms wrapped over his head. The hollowness of his face stole the breath from Azalea's lungs.

"Azzy, put more lavender on the fire," said her father. "I'll fetch some water."

The girl unhooked a bundle of flowers from the wall.

"W-what's happened to him?" she asked.

"I dunno," said Rosa-Lea, her face pale. "I found 'im like this at first lightness and I asks him, what's 'appened, son, what's wrong? But he don't say nothin'. He just lies there." She turned to Aspen. "It's the sickness, en't it? I can't lose 'im, Aspen, not after what 'appened to my Lea."

"No-one's losing anyone," he replied.

Azalea's father brought a clam-shell of water to Oak-Lea's lips and tipped it gently. The boy gulped at the liquid like medicine, until the grass doorway parted and Ceanotha swooped into the room.

"No water," she instructed. Azalea's mother rushed in behind her. "It will dilute the medicine. Marjoram, warm this on the fire."

She passed a third dose of the root to Azalea's mother. The vein of the plant darkened in the heat of the flames, then Marjoram tore it in half and offered a piece to Azalea.

"I don't need it, Ma," she said. "Let Oak-Lea have it."

"There's enough for both of you. Please, Azalea, just

take it."

Marjoram forced it into her hand then she sat down next to Oak-Lea. She broke off a bite-sized portion and placed it close to his mouth. The boy's lips locked shut like a limpet-crab.

"It'll make you better," said Marjoram. "Just try it, Oak-Lea, please."

The boy's eyes fixed on Azalea's face and he held her gaze for a long moment. She remembered what Ceanotha had said last darkness – *if a few lives must be sacrificed for the good of our people, then so be it* – and a feeling of panic grew in her chest.

"I have something to say!" she blurted, much louder than she had intended. "I, erm, I didn't eat my last piece of plant root. I threw it into the ocean."

Aspen lowered his eyebrows.

"Azalea," her mother said, gently, "thank you for being honest, but we'll talk about this later. We need to concentrate on Oak-Lea right now."

"You don't understand, Ma. What I'm saying is, Oak-Lea's had more of the plant root than me and look at him – it's not doing him any good." She took a breath of preparation before saying her next sentence. "Perhaps it's the root that's making him sick."

Her father's eyebrows shot up into his hairline.

"I know you're only trying to help," said Marjoram,

"but Ceanotha has foraged this plant to make Oak-Lea better. She knows what she's talking about, Azalea."

"But it's *not* making him better. There weren't nothing wrong with him and now he's sick. If he don't want it, you shouldn't make him. It's up to Oak-Lea whether he eats it or not. Tell her, Pa."

Her father looked into the boy's eyes.

"I'm sorry, Azzy," he said, "that's not your decision to make. It's up to Rosa-Lea." He turned to the boy's mother. "Rosa-Lea, do you want him to eat it?"

"I, I dunno," she told him, "I can't think proper."

"Well, what would your Lea say?" he asked.

The whisper of a smile edged its way onto Rosa-Lea's face.

"He'd say, *the body wants what the body needs*. He'd say if our Oaks don't want it, it's because he don't need it. He wouldn't force 'im to eat that root, so I guess I won't neither."

A surge of spirit rose up in Azalea. She snatched Oak-Lea's portion of the root from her mother's hand.

"Well, that's that then," she said. "Decision made," and without warning she threw both pieces into the fire.

"Azalea!" cried Marjoram.

Her mother stared at the flames in horror as the root crackled like a damp log.

Ceanotha's face flickered along with the fire-light.

"I fear you are making a grave mistake," she said.

But Rosa-Lea wasn't listening. She was bringing a shellful of water to her son's lips and stroking his head with the flat of her hand, and Azalea could see she was hardly aware there was anyone else in the room.

*

At suppertime, Azalea's mother demonstrated her anger by grinding corn with her knuckles and shelling beech-nuts with her teeth.

"You knew very well what Lea would've said," she snapped. Marjoram spat a nutshell into the bin. "He was always saying it. It doesn't mean he was right though."

"He wasn't *always* saying it," muttered Aspen. Marjoram looked as if she might throw something at him. "Oh, look how dark it's getting outside," he said, his eyes bulging. "Come on, Azzy, it's time you and me went to the lavender-harvest," and they left the tree before Marjoram pushed them out of it.

The forest roof shone with the glow of lavender as they walked towards the grassway. It pushed down through the slatted floors of the neighbouring homes, throwing shadows over their heads. Azalea could hardly wait for the chance to talk about what had happened.

"That plant root's poisonous, Pa!" cried the girl, once her mother was well out of earshot.

He picked a long strand of grass, pinched the stem and slid his fingers to the top, removing the seeds and scattering them over the ground as they walked.

"Yes, I think it is."

"Why would Ceanotha want to hurt me and Oak-Lea? First she got Bryony to trap us inside the mechanicary house, then when we didn't catch the Sapien sickness, she fed us a poisonous root instead."

"I think there's more to it than that," he replied. "I think Ceanotha knew full well you wouldn't catch the Sapien sickness from the ruin. I think the only reason she shut you in there was so she had an excuse to feed you that root."

"I don't understand," she said. "How could Ceanotha be so sure we wouldn't catch the sickness?"

"Think about it, Azzy. If you were hiding something in the woodland, something you kept underneath a secret doorway at the other end of the mechanicary house tunnel, wouldn't inventing a story about an ancient sickness be a great way to stop anyone finding it?"

"You think she made it up?"

"Well, Thornton Vine didn't die of the sickness and Ceanotha's lying about Oak-Lea having it too, so how much evidence do we have that the sickness even exists?"

"There's Iris Green," she replied. "She caught the Sapien sickness from the chamber below the mechanicary house and then—" Azalea gasped, remembering something from a previous conversation. "Iris Green ate the same plant root. Ceanotha told me so herself. You don't think that's why she…"

The girl couldn't finish that sentence.

She stared at the woodland. The tangled trees curled like smoke in the light of a low half-moon.

"Azzy," said Aspen, "I want you to go home. Tell your mother you weren't feeling well so I sent you back."

"Why, what are you going to do?"

"If Ceanotha is hiding something important enough to poison my daughter for, I'm going to find out what it is."

"No, Pa, it's too dangerous." He was already walking towards the trees. "Pa, I really don't think you should do this."

"Go," he instructed, without looking back.

Azalea watched him step over the thorned rope of the woodland. Her heart quickened. What if Ceanotha was there again? What if she was angry with him for snooping around in the restricted area? What if she did the same to her father as she did to Iris Green? What if he disappeared and she never saw him again?

With her heart in her mouth, Azalea sped along the grassway, over the rope and into the woodland. Her father was nowhere in sight, so she picked her way through the brambles in the same direction they had taken before, and found him searching the ground of the clearing.

"Pa," she hissed.

Aspen almost jumped out of his skin.

"Azzy, I told you to go home. I'm serious, get out of here."

"If you won't let me go down there with you," she said, "at least let me keep a look-out."

"No. No way. It's not happening. Go home, Azzy."

"*Please*, Pa, I'm frightened." She looked desperately into his eyes, her vision lighting his face. "I just want to know you're okay."

He sighed, worriedly.

"Fine," he relented, "but if anything goes wrong, anything at all, run back to the tree and tell your mother. Do *not* come looking for me, Azzy, do you hear me?" and Azalea nodded.

A blanket of ivy carpeted the ground like an autumn

mist. Her father pulled it to one side and a small, round doorway appeared. The hole was sealed with a metal disc. Aspen picked up a stick, placed it against the metal and levered it open.

"I won't be long," he told her, as he lowered himself into the tunnel.

His eyes lit the inside of a narrow hole, where a set of vertical climbing-steps reached down into the darkness. Azalea could hear his feet on the metal rungs as he moved into the ground and soon his vision became swallowed up by the shadows.

She waited impatiently in the darkness, twisting her hair around her thumb. A log-owl hooted. The buzz of dark-flies hovered somewhere nearby. A grey-fox scuttled past with her young. He said he wouldn't be long. Where *was* he?

Azalea peered into the hole.

"Pa?" Her voice bounced down the passageway. "Is everything all right, Pa?"

The girl shivered. She had promised not to go after him, but how could she leave him down there on his own? She would rather break her promise and make sure he was safe, than keep it and risk losing him.

At the mouth of the tunnel, Azalea dangled her feet into the hole. The passage had not been built for someone Azalea's size. Her shoulders were too broad to move comfortably through it and her back scraped against the cold brick wall, until a familiar smell of damp flooded her nose and her dark-vision started to flicker.

There was a light below her.

Azalea stepped onto a damp floor and ducked her head out of the tunnel. Her father was standing underneath a stone archway. He had his back towards her and his body was blocking her view of the room beyond.

"Pa," she said, gently. He turned numbly, only half-surprised. "What is it?"

Aspen opened his mouth to answer but no words came out, so he stepped to one side instead.

A cylindrical tower of swirling light occupied the centre of the chamber. It was profoundly radiant like sky-stars and pure white like the jewels of the Crystal Shore. She had never seen anything like it, yet somehow the light felt like coming home, as if it had always been there, as timeless as the land itself, as endless as the ocean, and Azalea felt drawn to it like a hawk-moth to a flame.

The pulse of the light synchronised with the beat of her heart as she walked towards it.

"What *is* it?" she asked, unable to pull herself away.

"I don't know," said her father. "Look at that

shadow."

A silhouette was moving inside the light's liquid walls. Azalea studied it with interest. It looked like a tiny figure, no taller than a newborn baby but walking around in the brightness. Then the light started to drone. It was a thick and heavy noise, one that arrived suddenly and filled the room with urgency, as the figure inside it started to grow.

Aspen shouted something from beneath the din, dragging her towards the climbing-steps. Azalea seized hold of the rails and turned to look over her shoulder. The figure was almost life-size. It hung in the watery surface like a ghost, pale clouds turning under its skin as its face burst out from the light.

"*Climb!*" bawled her father, and Azalea couldn't tell if the walls of the tunnel were shaking or if the shuddering came from inside her, as she scrambled out of the hole, tore through the woodland and ran all the way to the village without looking back.

At the roots of her tree, she heaved great lungfuls of cool air into her body, scanning the forest as a sickening emptiness filled her stomach.

Her father was nowhere in sight.

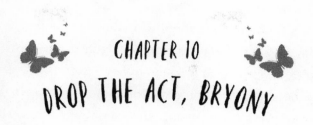

CHAPTER 10
DROP THE ACT, BRYONY

Azalea climbed to the fourth branch and ran into her mother's sleeping-hut.

"Ma!" she cried. "Ma, wake up!"

Marjoram rubbed the sleep from her eyes.

"Azalea? Why aren't you at the lavender harvest?"

"He was behind me," she said. The words flew from her mouth like fruit-bats out of a cave. "But when I turned around, he wasn't there and—"

The grass doorway burst open and Aspen fell breathlessly into the hut.

"Here I am," he panted, managing a smile. "Panic over." From the pocket of his leaf-shirt, he produced a handful of red-currants. "I stopped past the grove on the way back from the harvest. Sorry, Azzy, I thought you'd seen where I was going," and Azalea forced a smile too.

"It's all right," she said, her voice trembling. "I thought perhaps that's where you were."

Marjoram narrowed her eyes.

"I'm not sure which one of you I trust the least." She thought about that for a moment. "Azalea, I don't want you going to the lavender harvest anymore. You can stay here with me instead. I'll be watching you like a hawk-eagle from now on." Her eyes turned to Azalea's father. "You too, Aspen Fern," she added.

He looked at his feet like a scolded child, then the two of them climbed quickly down to Azalea's branch as Marjoram went back to her bed.

"Where *were* you?" Azalea hissed. "That light, the face… I was scared."

"You're quicker than me," he told her, "so I laid low in the woodland until I was sure we weren't being followed. I hid in a red-currant bush until the coast was clear."

"I couldn't get out of there fast enough. What did we just see, Pa? Who was that person in the light?"

"I don't know, Azzy, but whoever it was saw *us* as clearly as we saw *them*, and if they tell Ceanotha we were down there…" His voice trailed off. "Let's concentrate on getting Oak-Lea better for the next few lightnesses. We can decide what to do about all this once we know he's okay. Get some sleep now, Azzy, and try not to worry. You must be exhausted," but Azalea felt sure she would never sleep again.

Spring was turning to summer, and the rising heat signalled the start of the fruit harvest. The orchards became drenched in colour: crimson polished cherries, sun-yellowed pears and auburn peaches, dappled with deep violet berries and indigo plums. The scent of it perfumed the air like lavender.

Azalea wanted to pick something for Oak-Lea. He had felt better these last few lightnesses, but he was still confined to his tree and could not harvest for himself. Azalea spotted a ripe fir-kiwi at the top of a young tree, so she climbed up to the first branch, stood on her tiptoes and...

The tree shook violently. Azalea tumbled onto the grass, dropping the kiwi and thumping her shoulder on a rock. The fruit rolled away. It stopped at the feet of Bryony Vine, who picked it up and took an enormous bite out of its furry skin.

"You want to be careful," she said. "That branch looks a bit wobbly to me."

"Go away, Bryony," snarled Azalea. "I don't want to talk to you."

"Oh, but I haven't seen you for *ages*," cooed the girl. "I've missed our little chats. What've you been up to lately? Gone into any deadly ruins? Caught any ancient sicknesses?"

Azalea avoided her gaze.

"Where I go has got nothing to do with you," she said.

Bryony gaped at the guilty look on her face.

"You *have*, haven't you? Wow, Azalea, you really are as stupid as you look. Apart from the fact you could die, going into the restricted area is an insult to the memory of my father and if you don't start showing more respect, I'll tell my grandmother you've been in there again."

"The memory of your father? Drop the act, Bryony, it's embarrassing."

"There's nothing *funny* about my pa being dead."

Azalea knew she should walk away from this conversation. Telling Bryony she had seen her father would be senseless, dangerous even. But, oh, how she wanted to wipe that smug grin off her face!

Azalea pulled herself up to her tallest height.

"I *know*, Bryony," she sneered.

"Know what?"

"I saw him, in the woodland. I saw him with my own two eyes, so there's no point in denying it. I know your father's alive, Bryony, and I know your family are a pack of liars. You can't squirm your way out of this one, so don't even try it."

The girl's smile melted. She didn't reply at first, and when she did, her eyes shone with wetness.

"What you said about my mother was bad enough," she uttered, her voice breaking, "but this is just cruel."

Azalea froze. She looked carefully into the girl's eyes.

"You didn't know."

"I didn't *know*, because it's not *true!*" shouted Bryony, and throwing the fir-kiwi onto the grass, she ran from the grove.

Azalea growled with frustration. How could she have been so stupid? Why couldn't her mouth stop talking when her brain told it to?

To avoid telling her father what she had done, Azalea stayed out for the rest of that lightness. When she finally arrived home, Marjoram was there too. It was the perfect excuse not to mention it, so she ate her supper in silence then went to bed early, where she lay awake for a long while, worrying about what she had said.

Time passed slowly, but shortly after mid-darkness Azalea drifted into a vivid dream. She was back in the woodland and the figure was pushing its way out of the light. It burst through the watery surface in a fiery rage, a deep scar marking the place where its left eye had once been, and took hold of her by the throat. Azalea pulled herself free and ran to the tunnel, but the climbing-ladder had gone, so she hammered her fists on the walls of the chamber, shouting for someone, for anyone, to help her.

Bang, bang, bang…

Azalea sat bolt upright in bed, gasping for air. Something was hitting the wall of her sleeping-hut. She pulled back the shutter and peered down through the darkness to find Bryony at the foot of her tree.

"Rowan and my grandmother have gone to the lavender harvest," she said, without explaining her sudden appearance. "They go there all the time, but they don't always bring flowers home. Do they know?"

"Look, Bryony, about what I said to you earlier, I was just—"

"*Do they know?*" she repeated. Azalea nodded. "Show me," demanded the girl.

"I can't *show* you, Bryony."

"Yes, you can. You said he was in the woodland, so that's probably where they are now. Show me, or I'll howl for your mother and tell her everything."

Azalea seethed quietly out of the window, then she climbed down from her sleeping-hut and stormed through the forest towards the grassway, where a thin mist covered the ground like a fallen cloud.

"I en't happy about this," she grumbled, as they entered the woodland. "I don't like being blackmailed, Bryony, and we don't even know if they're here." She looked sideways with a raised eyebrow. "You en't got your dark-vision then yet?"

Bryony pulled a face in response.

"No," she said, "and we all know what an achievement it is to have shiny eyeballs, don't we?"

They carried on in silence until the scent of sweet-coriander drifted towards them. Azalea dropped to her hands and knees, then they crawled to the other side of the foliage and parted the leaves. Three pairs of eyes lit the clearing. Ceanotha and Rowan were facing them, but all they could see of Thornton was the back of his head.

Bryony looked nervously at Azalea, then back to the clearing.

"The arrival has been brought forward," said Thornton. "Parvan and her people will be here in two lightnesses."

"So soon?" asked Ceanotha. "I thought preparations were still being made."

"They are, but Parvan came to assess the woodland for building materials and found two people in the underground chamber. A young girl and an older male."

Azalea's stomach churned. She was sure they would hear her pounding heart hitting the ground of the woodland.

"Two guesses who *that* was," muttered Rowan.

"I thought you'd secured the area," Thornton went on. "Did you put up a boundary-fence like I asked?"

Ceanotha's nostrils flared.

"Are you questioning me again, Thornton Vine?"

At the sound of his name, Bryony gasped. The weathered female heard the intake of breath and turned her dark-vision towards the bush. Azalea pressed her face into the dirt to avoid the light.

"Who goes there?" she barked. "Show yourself!"

Bryony stood up. She walked out from her hiding place with her chin held high and Thornton's face softened as his eyes fell on his daughter.

"Bryony?" he gaped.

"How *dare* you follow us like this?" snapped Ceanotha. "Go back to the tree immediately!"

"No," said the girl, her voice loud but wavering. "Not until you tell me what's going on. Not until you explain why you've told such a terrible lie."

"I'm sorry, Bryony," her father said, gently. "We planned to tell you once you were old enough. Now I see how much you've grown, I realise we've waited too long."

"Don't confuse height with maturity," scoffed Rowan.

Bryony rounded on him.

"And how long have *you* known about this?" she growled.

"Ages," shrugged the boy, "and you would've known too if you could keep your mouth shut." He turned to their father. "I guarantee the whole village will know you're alive before sunrise."

"They will not!" yelled Bryony.

"None of us will have to keep it a secret for long now," their father interjected, "and Bryony deserves to know the truth before the others."

"Thornton," began Ceanotha, shaking her head, "I think it's best we don't say too much."

"It's fine, Mother." His eyes were fixed on his daughter. He held out his hand. "Come with me, Bryony, and I'll explain everything," and Azalea watched through her fingers as the four of them disappeared into the hatch.

CHAPTER 11
YOU WERE THERE

"Is something wrong?" asked Azalea's mother. The girl lowered her eyebrows. "You haven't said two words since you got up."

"Oh, it's nothing. I'm worried about Oak-Lea, that's all."

That *wasn't* all she was worried about, but her mother seemed to accept it.

"Why don't you visit him?" she said. "Don't stay long though, in case you catch something. You can give this to Rosa-Lea while you're there." She passed Azalea a newly-made leaf-dress. "It's a more suitable length than her other one. Howl loudly when you arrive and if you see Flora Elm's nose, tell her it was me who made the dress. It might make up for her seeing that boy spit a slug at me."

The walk to Oak-Lea's tree was a welcome distraction from the events of yesterlight. The heat was sweltering, even in the shade of the trees. Ground-rats and field-hares scampered into the shadows, while hook-sloths and tree-bears moved lower into the branches. Even the old cow-bull had entered the forest to keep cool.

Azalea howled at the roots. As usual, something dropped from the branches.

SPLAT!

It wasn't a slug, it was a dollop of tree-sap. It landed on Marjoram's new dress and slid down the front of it like a swamp-pig's sneeze. Flora Elm's nose immediately appeared at the window, as Azalea scurried up the trunk to avoid being seen.

She found Rosa-Lea stirring a pot of grain in the living-hut. Four pairs of hungry eyes watched the spoon as it turned, while Sycamore-Lea sat in a corner, pushing a ball of tree-sap up his nose.

"Azzy!" beamed Rosa-Lea, when she saw her arrive. "Come on in."

"Ma made this for you. Sorry about the sap. It was—" Sycamore-Lea's eyes grew large. "It was an accident," she finished.

"A bit of tree-sap never 'urt no-one," grinned the female. "Tell your ma I said ta very much. Our Oaks is still in 'is sleepin'-hut. He's a bit bored, if truth be told."

"I'll climb down and see him. I can't stay long though. Ma's worried I'll catch something." She rolled

85

her eyes. "You know what she's like."

Rosa-Lea put down her spoon and a mischievous look crept onto her face.

"Let me tell you somethin' about Marjoram Fern," she said. "When we were your age, Marj never did a flamin' thing she was told and she didn't care what other folk thought about it neither."

"We are talking about *my* mother, right?"

The female laughed.

"You remember me tellin' you about that fire-ants' nest? Your ma were bitten raw by them ants. She 'ad spots as red as a fruit-gibbon's backside, and when Primrose told Marj's mother where she'd got 'em, poor Marj weren't allowed out of 'er tree for seven whole lightnesses."

"Primrose Vine?" asked Azalea. "Bryony and Rowan's mother?"

"Aye, that's right. Your mother never did like 'er. She used to go buttermoth-catchin' with your father and I reckon Marj were a bit jealous. Anyway, point is, next time your mother tells you not to do somethin', just you mention that ants' nest and see what she 'as to say about it," and with a wink, she went back to her cooking.

Azalea knocked on the wall of Oak-Lea's sleeping-hut as she entered. A tall pile of twisted grass-string sat in the corner of the room. She pulled a fir-kiwi out of her pocket and threw it onto his lap.

"Thanks," he said. "Are you staying?"

"Course. What's with all the rope?"

"It's a lot, isn't it? Ma's going to make harvesting bags out of it. You can twist a lot of grass when you're stuck inside for five lightnesses. I'm so *bored*, Az."

An idea flew into Azalea's head. She took a handful of string and shoved it into her pocket. She pictured her mother halfway up the side of a fire-ants' nest, then she marched towards Oak-Lea and placed one hand under each of his arm-pits.

"Erm, what're you doing?" he asked.

"Taking you out," she said, hauling the boy to his feet.

"You know I can't walk, right?"

"It don't matter. I'm going to help you. Come on, forest-sloth, make an effort."

Azalea heaved him onto her back, climbed down from the tree and carried him all the way to the marsh-pond, where she sat him at the edge of the pool with his feet dangling into the cool water.

"I've done something stupid," she told him, "and it's really, *really* bad." She took a breath. "I accidentally told Bryony about her father being alive."

"How do you *accidentally* tell someone their father's

not dead?"

"That's not the worst of it either," she went on. "Bryony came to my tree during darkness and asked me to show her. So, we went to the woodland and Thornton was there with Ceanotha and Rowan, then they all went into the hatch together."

"What, Bryony too? Is she all right?"

Azalea shrugged.

"Ceanotha wouldn't hurt her own granddaughter," she said, doubting her own words. "But maybe I'll check on her later, just to make sure. Did you tell your ma about the root yet?"

"No," he replied. "I'm not going to mention it until we're certain it's true, or it might cause *even more* trouble between us and Ceanotha. You know what my ma's like."

She nodded.

"Oh, by the way, I had an idea about your legs. Wait there."

Azalea ran into the surrounding bushes and found two fallen branches. Then she brought them back to the pond, where she held them up against Oak-Lea and took the string out of her pocket.

"This might be none of my business," he said, as she tied the sticks to his legs, "but what are you doing?"

"Making you better," she told him. "There. Stand

up and see if it works."

Taking hold of his hands, Azalea pulled the boy to his feet. The branches kept him upright, but he wobbled like a newborn field-giraffe. She helped him over to the moss-covered log and fetched a second pair of sticks.

"Lean on these when you walk," she said. "Take it slowly though. We don't want you getting poisoned *and* breaking your neck all in one season."

The boy made his way unsteadily along the side of the water.

"I'm doing it," he said. "Look, Az, I'm doing it."

"Well, you en't gunna win no races," she told him, "but then you never won any races when you *could* walk." He stuck out his tongue in response. "Do you want to practise on the grassway?"

At the edge of the forest, they found Oak-Lea's ma and brothers playing with pine-cones. Rosa-Lea saw him from a distance and went mad with joy, her arms and legs flailing around like a crane-moth caught in the lavender smoke.

"My boy!" she cried, scrubbing him so hard on the head he almost fell over. "You're walkin' again! Azalea Fern, you're a bleedin' genius. En't she a bleedin' genius, Oaks?"

"She's all right," said the boy.

A pine-cone whistled past Azalea's ear. It smacked the smallest Moss child on the head and he spun around in search of the perpetrator. Rosa-Lea hoisted Sycamore-Lea off the ground by the roots of his hair and held him out at arm's length, where the boy snarled and growled like a young panther.

"Friends like 'er don't grow on trees, Oak-Lea," said Rosa-Lea, her train of thought not broken in the least. "Just you remember that, my lad. Do you wanna come back for some lunch, Azzy?"

"Thanks," said the girl, "but I've got to go somewhere. I'll see you all soon though," and she headed into the forest.

Azalea walked slowly through the trees. Checking on Bryony was the right thing to do, even though she was the most irritating person in the world, but how would she explain her visit if Ceanotha was home?

She stopped a short distance away from the tree to think-up an excuse.

"Can I help you?"

Startled, she looked up. Rowan was straddling the lowest branch, hollowing a nut-bowl with a sharpened flint.

"Oh, hi," she said, her face flushing. "Is Bryony in?"

The boy swept his white hair from his face and tilted his head like a crow-parrot.

"Why do you want to see Bryony?"

"I…I wondered if she wants to go swimming."

The boy scowled.

"But you hate each other."

"Well, yes, but Oak-Lea en't well enough to swim so I just thought…" This wasn't working. Rowan was right – Azalea would never invite Bryony to her marsh-pond. "You know what? Forget it. It was a stupid idea. I'll go on my own."

Rowan leapt from the branch. He landed in a crouched position at her feet, placed the sharpened flint into his pocket and stood up.

"Why are you *really* here, Azalea?"

He was standing too close for comfort.

"Can you move please?" she said. "You're in my way." The boy took hold of her wrist. "Hey, let go of me! That hurts!"

He moved his face closer to hers.

"You were there, weren't you?" he said. "You were in the woodland last darkness. *That's* how Bryony knew where we were. I bet you'd seen us in there before when you were snooping around near the hatch."

"I said *let go!*"

Azalea snatched her wrist away, pushing the boy hard on the chest with her other hand.

"I should've cut that creeper when you and the Moss boy were climbing out of the mechanicary house," he told her. "*That* would've put a stop to your nosiness."

Azalea's brow furrowed.

"It was *you* who told Ceanotha we climbed on the mechanicary."

"I was checking Bryony had done her job properly." He lifted his chin with menace. "I'm not sure how much you know, Azalea, but if you tell people about anything you've seen in the woodland, anything at all, there'll be consequences. Make sure you remember that," and as the boy climbed back to his branch, Azalea hurried away.

CHAPTER 12
DON'T LET GO

Azalea lay on the bed of the marsh-pond, looking up through the clear water at the sparkling sunlight. A silver-ray drifted over her stomach. She took it into her arms and lifted it to the surface, where it floated weightlessly as she stroked its smooth, rippling back.

"You know that's weird, right?"

The voice startled both her and the ray.

"For field's sake, Bryony, why are you sneaking up on me like that?"

"You came to my tree," said the girl. "I was there. I heard you talking to Rowan. Did you come to apologise?"

Azalea screwed-up her nose.

"What've I got to apologise for?"

"For telling me about my father," she said. "If you hadn't opened your big mouth, Azalea, I wouldn't have gone to that chamber, I wouldn't have seen what I saw and *I wouldn't know what I know!*"

Her voice had become panicked, frenzied even.

Azalea pulled herself out of the water.

"You're talking about the light, aren't you?"

"I'm talking about *everything*," she said, suddenly close to tears. "I need to tell someone or my head's going to explode. It's not *just* the light, Azalea, it's... I need to show you."

"No way. I en't going into that woodland again. Ask someone else."

"Do you think I'd be asking *you* of all people unless I was desperate? You're the only person who knows about my father and you owe me. I wouldn't know anything about the stupid woodland if it wasn't for you."

Azalea scowled.

"Is this a trick?"

"I wish it was. Are you coming or not?" and she marched towards the boundary.

Curiosity burnt in Azalea's chest like a flame. As she watched Bryony step over the thorns, the fire inside her roared like thunder. She squeezed the water out of her hair, promised herself this was the very last time she'd go anywhere near the restricted woodland, and ran after her into the trees.

They made their way past the mechanicary house and towards the hatch. Bryony picked up a stick and levered open the doorway. Then they climbed down the steps and ducked out onto the damp floor, where the pulse of the light joined with the thumping of Azalea's heart.

Its brilliance stole her breath. The light glittered like moonshine on water, reflecting the grey walls of the chamber with jewel-like beauty as Bryony walked towards it and stared into the watery surface.

"Was it made by the Sapiens?" asked Azalea.

"No," said the girl, "but it holds the story of their extinction. Look closer and you'll see it."

Confused, Azalea did as she asked. At first she saw nothing, but soon an image emerged. Tiny people were moving around inside it. Not shadowy figures like the one she had seen with her father, but fully-formed people with faces and clothes, wandering around like living pictures. Azalea could see every hair on their heads.

Landscapes appeared under their feet. Trees and plants sprouted up from the earth, and fields of green and yellow swathed the ground. Some of the figures sowed seeds, then fruits blossomed and flowers bloomed, and the glorious land glowed with life.

A mechanicary rolled down one of the hills and buildings appeared. Not the crumbling ruins of Azalea's world, but newly built structures of red brick and grey slate, breathing white smoke into the sky and spewing liquid into the ocean.

"Those people are Sapiens," said Bryony. "Do you see that cloud?"

Azalea inspected a dark fog that was moving over the land.

"Yes. What is it?"

"It's called **pollution**," she answered. It was the first time Azalea had ever heard that word and it sent a chill down the back of her neck. "It came from the Sapien mechanicaries and buildings. It killed the harvests and poisoned the ocean, until the world became a place to survive, not to live."

As if having heard her voice, the Sapiens grew thin and weak. Their bones were visible under their skin, their eyes grew large and sunken, until suddenly, with a bright flash of orange, they were gone.

Azalea watched as the broken world smouldered its pain to the dying sun, and a lump formed in her throat.

"What was that?"

The light danced across Bryony's face like fire-flies.

"It was the Last **War**. It almost caused their extinction."

"What's a war?" asked Azalea. "And where are you getting all these strange words from?"

"They're Sapien words," she told her, "and a war is

when a species battles against itself. Pollution spoiled the earth. Nothing could grow, so the Sapiens fought each other for food until the final explosion of the Last War revealed the light. One moment this was just a dark mechanicary tunnel, and the next it glowed like the sun.

"By then, only a few Sapiens remained, but the land was lifeless and bare. They couldn't live where they were and the light became their only hope of survival." She moved closer to its dazzling surface. "Every pull of every tide, every turn of every season, are all because of this light. The Sapiens call it the **Gateway**."

Footsteps sounded on the metal climbing-steps above them. Bryony started to panic.

"We can't be seen," she hissed, desperately. "I wasn't supposed to tell anyone. If my grandmother finds out you know… We have to hide."

"But there *is* nowhere!" said Azalea, frantically searching the room. Bryony snatched hold of her hand. "Wait, what are you doing?"

"Don't let go," she said, and together they plunged through the shimmering wall of the light.

CHAPTER 13
WHAT ARE YOU DOING HERE?

To move through the skin of time is like pushing your face through a jelly-fish.

The thought floated like dandelion-fluff into Azalea's head. She had no idea why. In fact, she did not so much *think* the thought as spectate it. Was there somebody holding her hand? Their palm felt pale and wispy, like a faded star in a cloudy sky. A distant memory said she should not let go of it, so she tightened her grip and together they drifted towards a dimmer part of the light.

Her face burst through the warm membrane. Azalea tumbled out of the Gateway and onto a stone floor, where Bryony let go of her hand. They looked at each other, shocked and breathless. The light was still there, looking just as it did before, but the room was different.

"Quick," said Bryony, clambering to her feet, "we have to hide!"

She followed the girl through an open doorway and

into a second room. It was a long, narrow passageway, with a high ceiling and a flecked floor. At the far end, a tall window allowed the sunlight inside, and the two girls ran towards it in a bid for freedom.

Azalea placed both hands on its clear surface and stared out in confusion. Buildings towered in every direction. They formed a circle around a small patch of grass, where occasional plants grew out of large pots. Each structure had fifty or more windows and was twice the size of any tree in Midpoint Forest.

"Oh…my…fields," gasped Azalea.

She stared out at the buildings as if looking into a dream.

"When the last few Sapiens went into the Gateway," explained Bryony, "it took them to another place, somewhere they could survive."

"Another world, you mean?"

"No, this is the same world as ours, but it's a different season. The Gateway took the last Sapiens back in time so they could escape extinction, to an age when the land was unspoiled. Then the light faded and they've waited for the Gateway to reopen ever since."

"So this is…*the past?*"

Bryony nodded.

"My father said going into the light is like swimming against the current of time. It lets you travel

99

in the wrong direction and you finish off further up-stream than you started."

"Did you come here last darkness?"

"No," replied Bryony, "my father said it was too dangerous."

A figure walked out from one of the buildings. It was a female, but she was shorter than Oak-Lea and her hair was so fine you could see her scalp where it parted down the middle. Her forehead was tall, her cheeks were plump and her limbs were thin like wicker-stems. She wore clothes made from a strange, red material and her shoes had tiny platforms on the heels.

Behind her, a small, silver mechanicary appeared. An actual moving mechanicary, sliding along the ground like a giant land-slug. It stopped and a male got out. He was around the same height as Azalea and had no face-hair at all. He waved his arm for no obvious reason and the female did the same in return, then hand-in-hand they hurried into one of the buildings.

More figures appeared. Azalea pressed her face against the glass, unable to take her eyes off these strange creatures, when suddenly the window flew open like a doorway and she fell out onto the grass. She landed next to a plant-pot, one that was almost as big as herself.

Cowering behind it, she looked up at Bryony, whose face appeared suddenly frightened. She stepped further into the building and disappeared around the corner of the passageway. It looked as if she was hiding from someone.

Azalea gazed around her with wide eyes. One of the Sapiens, a male, no older than Azalea herself, had noticed the open door. He was walking towards it, heading straight for her, and before she could move he was right there next to her, no more than a step away. He hadn't noticed her trembling behind the plant-pot, but if he turned his head, he was bound to see her.

The boy swung the door closed. Then he turned away and moved towards an adjoining building, where he placed his hand on the wall of the entrance as Bryony reappeared behind her. The girl pushed on the clear surface, trying to let Azalea back inside, but the door wouldn't open.

Suddenly, a large shadow swept overhead. Azalea looked up. She couldn't see what had caused it, but a piercing cry shattered the quiet like ice. From out of nowhere, the tip of a skeletal wing skimmed the plant and a colossal bird landed on the grass in front of her.

Azalea had never seen anything like it. The bird was the size of a cow-bull, but thin and malnourished, its bones showing through its featherless skin like sticks.

The creature folded its lucent wings into bat-like points, turned towards Azalea's hiding place and tipped its head to one side.

She froze, her heart almost bursting out of her chest. The peak of the bird's skull crested as it paced towards the plant-pot. Azalea could hear its breath moving in and out of its nostrils and felt the point of its beak brush her shoulder as it parted the leaves.

Thunder sounded. The bird whipped its head around to look over its wings, and then, as quick as lightning and twice as bright, an explosion threw Azalea backwards into the wall of the building and the world went dark.

When she opened her eyes, the bird had gone, the grass smouldered with fire and a hideous smell hung in the air. The sound of the blast rung in her ears, as a second mechanicary sped along one of the pathways. Its metallic shell reflected the sunlight like water. It stopped, and a group of Sapiens got out. They pulled snake-like devices from the back of the mechanicary and sprayed water onto the fire, as more of their species emerged from the buildings to watch.

A noise sounded behind her. Bryony was still trying to open the door, now beating the flats of her hands against the unmoving frame. Azalea jumped to her feet. She couldn't stay here. There had to be another way back to the Gateway, and so, with a fearful glance towards Bryony, she hurried over to the adjoining building.

The Sapiens were too busy dealing with the fire to notice her run up a short flight of climbing-steps to a closed wooden door. She tried pushing it open without success before noticing a box on the wall.

Remembering the boy, she placed her hand onto the strange contraption. The box made a noise like a field-cricket, but the door remained closed. She repeated the action again, and again, more urgently now with every attempt, until the door opened and there in front of her, no more than a breath away, stood the Sapien boy.

His expression was not one of fear, but one of curiosity, as if trying to identify a buttermoth or a fish. He stepped out of the building.

"Hello," he said, the idea of a smile flickering over his lips. "What are you doing here?"

Azalea was about to respond when something struck her between the shoulder blades, pushing her into the boy. He stumbled down the steps as she fell into the building, where the door slammed closed behind her.

CHAPTER 14
WE NEED TO TELL SOMEONE

"When you've finished chatting with the Sapiens, can we concentrate on getting back to the Gateway?"

Azalea turned to see Bryony standing behind her.

"Fields, Bryony, what did you do *that* for? And how did you get out of the other building?"

"The door just opened all of a sudden. I must've pressed the right part, I think. I was going to shout over to you, but I saw you needed rescuing, so—"

"I didn't need *rescuing*."

"That's not what it looked like to me. Anyway, we can't go back out there now, not with that Sapien boy waiting for us. But this building joins onto the other one, so there must be a way through."

"I already know that," snapped Azalea. "Why'd you think I came over here?"

They ran along a narrow walkway, through an arch and into a vast room. The size of it stopped the girls in their tracks. They had entered the very heart of the building, where the core of the enormous structure was hollow from top to bottom.

Azalea tipped back her head. Four long strands of Sapien-made lights hung down from the lofty roof and climbing-steps spiralled the walls like a tree-python, levelling off into platforms at regular intervals.

"Which way?" asked Azalea, scanning the room.

"The Gateway's in that direction." Bryony pointed to a door on the side wall. "We could try going through there, but if we see any Sapiens, try not to look so tall."

"And how am I meant to do *that?*"

Before Bryony could answer, the door opened. A Sapien walked into the room. She was talking to a small box on the back of her wrist, too engrossed in her conversation to notice them. But then, as Azalea tried to sink into her own legs, the female's gaze drifted across the room.

She stopped talking as her eyes landed on the two Homotium girls.

"Oh, no," Azalea murmured, hardly daring to move her lips. The female tapped carefully at the box with her finger, her eyes never leaving their faces. "What do we do?"

"I don't know," whispered Bryony. "Just don't make any sudden movements."

"But we have to do *something*. You saw what they

did to that bird. It could be us next. I can't believe your family were stupid enough to keep these creatures a secret from us."

Bryony gritted her teeth in response.

"Now's not the time, Azalea."

The female lowered her wrist. She smiled half-heartedly and then she just stood there, looking at them. Azalea could not help but notice how thin her legs were. She was pretty sure they could outrun her.

A crash sounded behind them and echoed around the room, as a second door was flung open. Scores of Sapiens scurried into the room like field-locusts, each wearing identical black clothing. Some of them carried peculiar metal objects, which they pointed at Azalea and Bryony as they formed a circle around them.

"Stay back!" shouted Azalea, her eyes darting from one face to another. "Don't come no closer!"

Only one of them seemed to hear what she said. He spoke to the others in words Azalea did not understand and the group stopped moving. He held up the palms of his hands, as if letting Azalea know he meant her no harm, then he pulled a silvery object from his pocket. It had two circular bracelets, linked together with a short chain.

He offered it to Azalea.

"What is it?" whispered Bryony.

"I dunno," she replied. "It might be a gift. Perhaps it's some kind of greeting. We don't want to offend them."

Carefully, Azalea stepped towards him. She held out her hands, allowing him to pick up her scent, and the Sapien lifted the object. He moved closer, slowly, their fingertips almost touching, and before she knew what was happening, he snapped the bracelets over her wrists and bound her arms like a rock-turtle caught in seaweed.

Terrified, Azalea pulled back her hands. She growled as she returned to Bryony's side, where she stared at her wrists in horror.

"Not a gift then," said Bryony. She looked up at the strands of lights. "Can you climb with that thing on your wrists?" Azalea nodded. "All right. Ready? *Now!*"

The Homotium girls leapt up and snatched hold of the creeper-like strings. One of the Sapiens called out to the others, as a cloud of panic fell over the room. They ran to the spiralling steps, their movements slow and awkward, as if running through water. By the time they had reached the first platform, the two girls were already level with the fifth.

"We need to get onto those steps," Bryony said, desperately. "Let's get further ahead so they can't catch up, then swing ourselves over to the rail."

The sound of Sapien feet bounced around the empty building like hail-fall, until, somewhere near the fifteenth floor, the girls stopped climbing. Bryony swung her light-strand towards the steps and a terrible thought came into Azalea's head. With her wrists tied, she couldn't reach out for the rail. She would have to let go with both hands and jump for it instead.

Bryony's feet brushed the steps, as a door on the landing slid open. It led into the tiniest room Azalea had ever seen and inside it was the Sapien boy.

"He followed us," wailed Bryony, abandoning her plan. "What're we going to do?"

The boy ran to the railing.

"Can you get to the **banister**?" he asked. Azalea didn't know what a banister was, but it seemed like he meant the rail. "If you swing over here, I will hide you from the **Enforcement**."

Azalea studied him carefully. His face looked puffy, as if having been stung by bees, and his skin was freckled like Oak-Lea's.

"How come he knows the same words as us and the big ones don't?" she asked Bryony.

"I don't know," replied the girl, "but I don't trust him. Come on, let's keep climbing."

The footsteps were growing louder by the heartbeat.

"I reckon he's harmless," said Azalea. "Plus there

108

are two of us and one of him, and, well, he en't no mud-lizard, Bryony." The boy eyed himself up and down, confused. "We can just push him over again if he tries anything."

Bryony scrutinised the boy like a strange beetle that just crawled out from a rock.

"Fine," she agreed. "You go first though."

This was typical of Bryony Vine, thought Azalea, as she swung her light-strand towards the platform. Always the first to point out other people's fears, and always the last to prove her own courage.

Azalea kicked out her legs in front of her. It was difficult to get any momentum on a rope of this length. She wasn't sure she could make it swing close enough to let go, but the sound of Sapien footsteps on the lower platforms spurred her on, until suddenly, with her heart in her mouth, she jumped.

She flew towards the platform, where her hands slapped onto the polished wood of the banister. Her white knuckles trembled as they gripped the rail, then her legs slammed into the side of the climbing-steps and the weight of her body pulled on her arms.

Her hands slipped. Bryony shouted her name as the rail slid past her fingertips. Azalea closed her eyes, not wanting to see what was happening, until a sudden jolt made the bracelets cut into her skin.

Breathless, she opened her eyes. The Sapien boy's face was an arm's length away from her own. His hands were holding the chain between her two wrists as she dangled from the fifteenth floor of the building. His arms shook, his cheeks were almost purple, then Bryony was there too and she pushed him to one side, shouting, "Give her to me!" before hauling Azalea over the rail and onto the safety of the platform.

She sat on the floor, visibly shaking.

"You have to hide," said the boy. "The Enforcement will be here any moment," and he ran back into the tiny room.

Azalea almost laughed.

"We en't hiding in there. There's only one door. If they find us, we'll be trapped."

"They will not find you," the boy replied, "but there is no time for me to explain. You will just have to believe me."

Azalea looked at Bryony, eyebrows raised.

"You're not seriously telling me you trust him?" she scowled.

"I trust him as much as I trust *you*," shrugged Azalea, and with a look of defiance, she followed him into the room.

Bryony went too, shaking her head. The door closed behind them and the Sapien boy pressed a circular shape on the wall.

The room grew suddenly unsteady, as if they were standing on a floating log, and when the door reopened Azalea found herself in a different place.

"Where are we?" she asked. She stepped out of the room and onto a higher platform. "Did we go through another Gateway?"

The boy smiled.

"No," he said, "we went in an **elevator**. Follow me."

Two rows of wooden doors lined the walls. He ran to the end of the line, took hold of a handle and pushed. Then he beckoned them inside before closing the door behind him.

The room was a similar size to Azalea's living-hut. A long seat made from a woven material occupied the far wall and a narrower version of the same object had been placed in one of the corners. A little white shelf stuck out from under the window, upon which someone had placed a jar of cut flowers. The floor was soft and thorn-rose pink, and the ceiling had three Sapien-made lights that illuminated the room with an unusual whiteness.

Azalea looked over to a second door as a voice came from behind it. A female stepped out. She was followed by a young girl, no more than twenty seasons old. The child was eating something purple on a stick and her mother was drying her hands on a small piece of material. When she looked up and saw the two Homotium, she dropped the cloth and ushered the child towards her.

The girl pulled away. She went over and held out the purple food. Azalea sniffed it, just as she did when Sycamore-Lea showed her a chewed dung-beetle, and the girl giggled. It was sugar-cane with a hint of black-currants.

"She is my sister," said the boy, "and this is my mother. Do not worry. They will not tell the Enforcement you are here."

He spoke briefly to his family in his own words. His mother smiled uncertainly, then she fetched a metal instrument from the adjoining room. It had two short blades, sharp enough to crack hazel-nuts with, and she handed it to the boy.

Azalea eyed it with caution.

"I will cut you free," he said, pointing at the ties on her wrists.

"Either that or he'll cut you up into little pieces so you're easier to digest," muttered Bryony.

The boy frowned.

"I do not know the meaning of 'digest.'"

"Don't worry about it," said Azalea. "She was trying to be funny. She does that a lot."

Azalea held out her wrists and the boy placed the instrument against the chain. The blades sliced through it like butter-milk, leaving the two bracelets hanging loose on her wrists and her arms free to move.

"How did you know about us?" he asked, putting the instrument down on a table. "My people think we are a secret from the Homotium."

"Thornton Vine is my father," said Bryony, shifting her weight, "so I know everything, including the fact you want to come back through the Gateway and live in our world."

Azalea's jaw dropped.

"*What?!*" she cried. She rounded on the boy. "You en't coming to our world with your fiery explosions and your mean fully-growns, pal, so forget it. Why can't you just stay here?"

"There are creatures in this time that are dangerous to us," he said. "We have been forced to build a wall around our homes to keep them out. This is why we must leave. We do not wish you any harm. In fact, Thornton has been teaching some of my species to speak your words, especially the younger generation, so we can communicate better with you once we arrive."

"If you're so harmless, why all the secrecy?" asked Azalea. "Why aren't we allowed to know about you?"

"The Homotium would be afraid and wish to stop our arrival," he said, "even though they have nothing to fear. My people thought it would be easier this way."

Footsteps sounded outside the room and somebody hammered on the door.

"It don't seem like there's nothing to fear," muttered Azalea.

The boy spoke to his mother and she pulled the young girl back into the adjoining room.

"If the Enforcement find out we have hidden you," he said, "my family will be in trouble. You must hide."

"We can do better than that." Azalea signalled to the window. "Does that thing open?"

"Yes, but you cannot escape through there. We live at the top of the **tower-block**."

"I dunno what that is and I en't got time to care. We'll be fine. Just open it please."

Hurriedly, the boy lifted a handle and the window-frame swung open. Azalea poked out her head. She could see the whole Sapien village from here. A hundred or more buildings were enclosed by a huge wall that encircled the settlement, and below her some of the Sapiens were still dampening the charcoaled grass. They were too busy to notice her climb out of the window and sit on the ledge.

"It is not safe," said the boy. "You will fall."

Bryony joined her on the window-frame.

"This might be high for *you*," said Azalea, "but we climb stuff like this all the time. Close the window behind us," and gripping the small indents of the brickwork, they began their descent.

The handholds and foot-crevasses between the bricks were tiny and by the time they reached halfway, Azalea's fingertips burned like fire.

"Please tell me you left that door open when you came out of the first building," she said to Bryony.

"Yes," she answered, "but what are we going to do if they see us?" and Azalea couldn't answer that question.

As they drew level with the fourth floor, some of the Enforcement filed out of the building. They scanned the ground for the two girls and fear grew quickly amongst the other Sapiens.

Then one of them looked up. His eyes met with Azalea's. He pointed at the wall, calling out to the others, as gradually, one by one, every face turned to look at her.

"*Run!*" cried the girl, and they leapt from the tower-block and onto the grass.

The Sapiens screamed as if two mud-lizards had landed amongst them. Some took hold of their children and ran into the buildings, others huddled together in groups, and at the same time the Enforcement charged towards them with their strange metal devices held out in front of them.

Something bee-like whizzed past Azalea's shoulder as she neared the door. There was no time to see what it was, so she shot into the building and along the tunnelling room, until the pulse of the Gateway joined with her heart.

The light shone quietly in the small room. Azalea snatched hold of Bryony's hand as they jumped towards it, where they drifted like clouds for a short while before landing heavily on the stone floor of the underground chamber.

Azalea knelt breathlessly for a moment, checking whoever was descending the climbing-steps earlier on had left.

"We need to tell someone," she gasped, scanning the empty room. "We need to tell *everyone*. We can't let the Sapiens into our world."

CHAPTER 15
STAY WHERE YOU ARE

They scrambled out of the undergrowth and onto the grassway, speeding towards Midpoint Forest at breakneck speed.

"Bryony, listen," puffed Azalea, as they stopped at the edge of the trees, "I know telling the village means going against your family and I know your pa might end up in trouble, but the Sapiens are dangerous. I don't reckon we have a choice."

Bryony glowered at the woodland, as if it was somehow responsible for this whole awful mess.

"My father didn't care about me for the last forty seasons," she said, "so why should I care about him now? I'll never forgive my family for helping that species come into our world."

Azalea felt she should say something helpful.

"Perhaps they did it to keep your family safe," she suggested.

Bryony curled her top lip.

"How is inviting a bunch of bird-killing monsters to live with us going to keep us safe?"

"Well, there must be *some* reason your family have done this. I bet the Enforcement will be a lot nicer to you than the rest of us because of their help." Bryony looked at the ground. A hint of embarrassment played on her face. "Do you reckon anyone will believe us?"

"I doubt it," she said. "It'll be our word against my grandmother's."

Azalea thought for a moment.

"My pa's seen the Gateway for himself. We could tell him first and he could explain it to the others. They'll be more likely to believe a fully-grown than us."

Bryony pulled a face.

"Aspen Fern? Really?"

"There en't nothing wrong with my pa, Bryony Vine," scowled Azalea, but she kind of knew what she meant. "Okay, so he's no Ceanotha Vine, but then who'd want to be? Come on, it's got to be worth a try."

Azalea's parents were preparing supper when they entered the living-hut. Marjoram's face looked like it was going to say something along the lines of, "Where've you been, Azalea? Why are you almost late home?" but seeing Bryony, her expression changed to one of sweetness and joy.

"Bryony, how lovely to see you," she cooed. "Do you want to stay for some supper? I'm making root-potatoes with—"

"She don't want no supper," blurted Azalea. "We've got something to tell you."

Marjoram fumed quietly from behind her smile, but Aspen noted the urgency in Azalea's voice.

"What is it, Azzy?" He spoke again when she couldn't quite find the words. "Is it about the light?"

"What light?" asked Marjoram.

Azalea paused. She hadn't realised how ridiculous it would sound until she tried to say it out loud.

"For field's sake," said Bryony, with impatience. She turned to Marjoram. "There's a light buried in the woodland. These two have both seen it." She nodded at Azalea. "Go on, tell her."

"It's...a Gateway to another world," she announced. "When you go into it, you travel back in time. It's like swimming against the current of something or another." She looked at Bryony. "What was it again?"

"Time," the girl finished. "It's like swimming against the current of time, so you finish off further upstream than you started."

Marjoram looked perplexed, yet still twittered like a bird with amusement.

"Very good," she chuckled. "Aren't you two a bit old for tree-pixie stories?"

Aspen's eyes were fixed on Azalea's face.

"Keep going," he said to her. "I'm listening."

"The Sapien discovered the Gateway when their species was almost extinct," she went on. "It took them to an ancient season and they've lived there ever since. Me and Bryony have been to their world. We've seen them for ourselves so we know it's true. The Sapien species is not extinct."

Marjoram stopped laughing.

"What is this, Azalea? Some kind of a joke? Only, it's getting a bit out of hand. Enough's enough."

Bryony took hold of Azalea's arm and showed it to Marjoram. The silvery ties were still on her wrists.

"The Sapiens made those," said Bryony. "There's this group called the Enforcement. They killed a bird and they tried to capture us."

"They're really dangerous," Azalea added, "and they're going to live here in *our* season. Bryony's family have been keeping their plan a secret ever since discovering the Gateway."

Her father absorbed the news like an ocean-sponge.

"When will they arrive?"

"Oh, Aspen, stop encouraging them," sniffed Marjoram.

120

"We don't know," replied Bryony, "but it's definitely soon. We want to warn the rest of the village, but we're worried they won't believe us."

Marjoram took the potatoes off the fire and placed the pan on a table.

"Supper's ready," she said. "Let's stop this nonsense and all have a nice bowl of—"

"We don't *want* no supper!" snapped Azalea. Marjoram's eyes swelled. "Please, Pa, say you believe us. We need your help to convince the rest of the village."

Aspen stared at the metal contraption on his daughter's wrists, then he stood up and paced the floor.

"You girls howl at every tree in the village," he said. "Tell them to go to the old tree-stump right away. Tell them it's urgent. I'll meet you there."

A pained look grew suddenly on Marjoram's face.

"Aspen, you're not serious?"

"There are things you don't know about, Marjoram. Things I should've told you before. If you'll just come with me to the tree-stump, I'll explain everything."

Marjoram slammed an eating-bowl down on the table.

"You mean you'll explain it to me and the rest of the forest. No, thank you," she said. "I'd rather stay here

121

and eat on my own than watch you humiliate us. You'll be a laughing stock, Aspen."

Azalea left the tree to the sound of her father still pleading with Marjoram. Most of the villagers were reluctant to leave their homes so close to darkness. But when Bryony lied and told them her grandmother had requested their presence, a crowd soon gathered on the forest ground.

Aspen was there waiting for them. He called for quiet as he stepped up to the old tree-stump and a confused silence pressed through the sound of their voices.

"There's something I need to tell you," he began. His face glistened in the light of their eyes. "There's something in the restricted woodland, something Ceanotha doesn't want any of us to find. She invented a story to keep us out of there, but it's time you all knew the truth." He swallowed hard. "The Sapien sickness doesn't exist."

There was muttering from the crowd, and then Rosa-Lea left the group to gently take hold of his hand.

"It's all right, Aspen," she said, trying to coax him down from his podium. "You're just a bit confused, that's all. It 'appens to all of us. My Oaks 'ad the Sapien sickness, do you remember, Aspen?"

Azalea glowered from the front of the group.

"He en't lost his acorns, Rosa-Lea. He's just trying to tell you something. Ceanotha fed poison to us. That's why Oak-Lea got sick. The same thing happened to Iris Green."

"Only more successfully," muttered Bryony, under her breath.

A voice called out from the back.

"You can't go throwing accusations like that around!" Flora Elm elbowed her way to the stump, nose first. "You should be ashamed of yourselves. Fancy saying all this when poor Bryony's standing right there in front of you. She lost her father to that sickness, you know."

"Actually," said Bryony, her voice factual and emotionless, "I didn't. My father's still alive."

The villagers started to whisper, but Flora Elm shook her head.

"Are you hearing this, everyone?" she asked, turning to face the crowd. "They've put all sorts of ridiculous fantasies into the poor girl's head. What sort of Homotium would knowingly cause such pain and anguish to another living soul?"

Azalea's whole body tensed at the sound of her words. It felt as if the anger would explode through her chest. She marched up to the tree-stump, bumping past Flora Elm on the way, and stood tall at the side of her

123

father.

"For your information, *Flora...*" She said the female's name as if the taste of it made her stomach churn. "...all three of us have seen Thornton Vine. Ceanotha's lied to you about his death and she's lied about the sickness too.

"There's a hatch," she went on, "in the woodland. It leads down to an underground chamber. It's part of a Sapien-built tunnel that starts at the mechanicary house and goes right underneath the trees. There's a light down there. Bryony's father told her it's a Gateway to the past. The Sapien's went through it and escaped extinction, and now they're coming here to our world."

Flora Elm laughed like a donkey.

"Did you hear that?" she hooted. "Aspen and Azalea have found a *time-mechanicary!* Oh, I can't *wait* to hear what Marjoram has to say about this."

The words had barely left her mouth when a figure dropped from above her. Its feet narrowly missed the female's nose as it landed in a crouched position on the forest ground.

Marjoram Fern stood up and straightened her leaf-dress.

"Well, you won't have long to wait," she said, "because I'll tell you what I think about it right now."

She walked to the tree-stump. Azalea tried to step down in order to make room for her, but Marjoram took hold of her arm. "No," she said, "stay where you are," and she turned to face the crowd.

"As you all know," began Marjoram, "I'm very strict about what my family can and can't do. Aspen doesn't go fish-catching anymore, he doesn't watch the buttermoths in the lavender field and he hasn't climbed the White Rocks since we were youngsters." She turned to face her partner. "We used to enjoy looking at the rock-puffins, but it's fair to say, I'm not an easy Homotium to live with lately."

"Oh, Marjoram," he said, "that's not true."

"It's a *bit* true," muttered Azalea.

Her mother heard her, and smiled.

"The point is," she went on, "Aspen and Azalea don't do things they know will upset me. Nothing they think I'll find out about anyway. And with that in mind, who here thinks either one of them would stand here making all of this up if it wasn't true?"

Rosa-Lea snorted.

"They wouldn't dare," she remarked, and the crowd mumbled its agreement.

Marjoram targeted Flora Elm with her stare like a log-owl eyeing a mouse.

"What's more," she said, "while I was sitting up

there on that branch listening to this whole conversation take place, I realised Aspen and Azalea have nothing to be ashamed of. It took courage to stand in front of you and say something they knew you might not listen to. But they did it because they believe it is true and they did it for the good of our people. I for one trust what they are saying, and I suggest anyone who doesn't asks Ceanotha for themselves."

At the sound of her name, the old female stepped out from the shadows like a spectre. She pushed the end of her staff into the soft earth, as if rooting herself to the spot.

"That won't be necessary," she said. "I'm here now and I shall explain everything."

Rosa-Lea seethed audibly through gritted teeth.

"It'd better be good," she snarled. "If Marj believes what Aspen and Azalea are tellin' us, then I believes it too. I know what you done to my boy, Ceanotha. What's Oak-Lea ever done to you though, eh?"

"He threatened the safety of our species," she replied, without expression. "I merely did what was necessary to ensure the future of our people."

Ceanotha scanned the crowd with hawk-like stillness and it seemed the forest held onto its breath.

"Everything Aspen and Azalea have told you is true," she announced. "I found the Gateway shortly after it appeared in the woodland, not long after Bryony was born. A figure stepped out of it. She is a Sapien and her name is Parvan. Her people used the light to escape extinction, but then it closed and they were abandoned in a time where they don't belong.

"Their knowledge is advanced and powerful. It makes them a dangerous and unpredictable species. This is why my family have made an alliance with them, to ensure the Homotium are safe. We promised to keep their existence a secret until they were ready to join our world and Parvan has assured our wellbeing in return." She glanced towards Rosa-Lea. "I've had to take drastic action so the alliance was not broken, but if I hadn't, our whole species would be in terrible danger and many more lives would be lost."

"And what if we don't *want* them to live here?" scowled Azalea. "I've been to their world, Ceanotha, and I've seen how dangerous they are."

The old female pulled her stick out of the ground.

"I should've known it was you who left the hatch open this lightness, Azalea."

"It wasn't *just* her," said Bryony, and her grandmother stared the girl in the eye for a long moment.

"You may protest if you wish," replied Ceanotha, "but it will make no difference. The first wave of

Sapiens will arrive at sunrise."

"Next lightness?!" cried Azalea. "But they can't! We won't let them!"

Ceanotha did not even look at her.

"Those who wish to join the alliance may come to the milking-cow field to greet them," the old female went on. "Those who wish to do otherwise, your safety is not guaranteed. Now, everyone get some sleep. We have a busy lightness ahead of us."

CHAPTER 16
IS THIS HOW IT'S GOING TO BE?

Azalea couldn't sleep. She listened to the muffled voices of her parents until shortly before sunrise, when they left their sleeping-hut and climbed to the topmost branch of the tree.

"We've been talking," said Marjoram, trying to hide the redness of her eyes as Azalea entered the hut, "and we've made a decision. All of us are going to the milking-cow field at sunrise."

"Good," said the girl. "We can tell the Sapiens we don't want them here."

Her father looked at Marjoram then back to his daughter.

"No, Azzy. We're going to join the alliance."

"You're not serious?" She looked at their faces and their eyes turned to the floor. "You can't. I won't."

"It wasn't an easy decision," her mother said, unable to look at her, "and we don't like it any more than you do. But we're your parents, Azalea. It's our job to keep you safe and we'll do whatever it takes to protect you."

"But I've been to their world, Ma. I've seen what they're like, especially the Enforcement. We can't let them live here."

"I don't see how we can stop them. Now, go and get ready – we want to get there on time."

The milking-cow field stretched from the eastern side of the lavender field to the foot of the Farnorthern Hills. It was home to thirty or more cattle, who kept the grass short and trimmed the hedgerow during summer.

From the top of the grassway, Azalea looked miserably out at the landscape. Other villagers were trailing down to the field in fearful silence. It seemed her parents were not the only ones who wanted to keep their children safe.

Several green huts had appeared in the milking-cow field over darkness. They were made from a woven material, one similar to the clothing worn by the Sapiens, and it flapped loudly in the breeze like rubber-plant leaves. A group of figures stood around them on the grass. Even from so far away, it was clear they were not Homotium.

Azalea's mother gasped and Aspen took hold of her hand.

"Take a breath, Marjoram. We'll stick together and it'll be fine, you'll see."

As they entered the pasture, Azalea realised the first wave of Sapiens were dressed in identical black clothing. The Enforcement had arrived and the sight of them made her skin turn icy.

Then Ceanotha Vine came out from one of the huts. Thornton was with her, and they were joined by a female Sapien. She looked older than Azalea's mother and her forehead was flat like a cliff-face. Her cheeks were round and her hair was cut into a neat bowl-shape, one Rosa-Lea Moss would have been proud of.

Thornton exchanged words with her as the group of Homotium entered the field. For most of them, it was the first time they had seen Ceanotha's son for many seasons. Even so, their eyes were pulled to the Sapien Enforcers, drinking them in like a sour-tasting liquid they had no choice but to swallow.

The Sapien female took a long-handled tool from one of the huts and approached the group.

"My name is Parvan," she told the Homotium. Her voice was too calm for comfort. "On behalf of the Sapien people, I wish to thank you for welcoming us into your season. Together we shall build a united world to benefit both of our species.

"First, we shall construct a central building called an

energy-house. It will bring light during darkness, warmth during winter and power for harvesting. In preparation for our arrival, my people have spent many seasons making building materials to bring through the Gateway. Some of us have been learning your **language** too. We shall surely build a better future now our worlds have come together," then she spoke quietly to Thornton, before going back into the hut.

"Follow me," he said to the Homotium. His eyes were turned to the ground, unable to look at the faces of the villagers he had not seen for so long. "I'll show you where to dig."

"Dig?" said Marjoram. "We came here to welcome the Sapiens and join the alliance, not to dig up a field."

Ceanotha stepped forward.

"You heard what Parvan said. The energy-house will be built first, so the **foundations** must be laid as soon as possible. Let's not anger the Sapiens on their first lightness in our world, Marjoram."

"What're foundations?" asked Azalea.

"They are the roots of a building," the old female replied. "You will dig holes for them around the edge of this field. The milking-cows will have a new home on the Farnorthern Hills, so the energy-house can be at the very heart of the land."

"Why can't the Sapiens go and live on the

Farnorthern Hills instead?" asked the girl. "Or better still, why don't they go and live on the distant land?"

Ceanotha responded with a steely glower.

"Do as Thornton told you and follow him," she said. "We have a lot of work to complete before sunfall," and the other Homotium were too frightened to disobey.

At the far edge of the field, a line of markers ran parallel to the hedgerow. The tools were handed out by some of the Enforcers, who watched the Homotium as they started to work. The weight of their eyes made Azalea feel awkward and uncomfortable, as she begrudgingly shovelled the earth.

After a while, more Sapiens came out of the woodland. They were not part of the Enforcement, Azalea could tell from the way they were dressed. They moved with wide eyes past the Homotium, as they came to remove the soil in wheeled barrows.

"Remind me why we're doing this again," Azalea said to her father, throwing yet another spade full of dirt out of the hole.

"Because we have to. We need to at least get the measure of this species before we refuse their requests, Azzy." Something in the earth caught his eye. "Everyone stop digging," he said, raising his voice. "There's a mud-millipede nest over here."

The news travelled quickly along the trench from

one Homotium to the next. They paused, as the Sapiens watched with quiet interest. One of the workers must have understood Aspen's words, because she pointed into one of the barrows with a face of disgust, then the others let go of the handles and moved away from the insects.

Azalea was about to go over and tell them to put the soil back where it came from, when a commotion on the northernmost side of the field drew her attention. Parvan was trying to coax the milking-cows through a gap in the hedgerow with the help of the Enforcement. The confused creatures were moaning in protest, which in turn alerted the old cow-bull from his spot near the grassway.

The weathered creature hoofed his way into the field and strode towards the herd, stamping his feet and snorting angrily. Parvan took a rope from her shoulder. She tossed it over his head and pulled the noose taut.

"Hey!" shouted Azalea, climbing out of the trench. "Don't do that! You're frightening him!"

The cow-bull broke into a frenzied dance, bucking his legs and scuffing up great chunks of grass with his thick hooves.

Azalea ran towards him. The rope cut into his neck as the end of it slipped through Parvan's fingers and the terrified beast saw his chance. He kicked out in a bid to escape. One of his back hooves pounded Parvan on the shoulder. She cried out and dropped to the ground, where she curled into a ball and covered her head with both arms.

"Keep still!" called Azalea, now sprinting as hard as she could. "He'll calm down if you don't move!"

One Enforcer snatched hold of the rope while the others swarmed around him. The old cow-bull butted him in the stomach with the front of his rock-like head. The Sapien doubled over, pulled a metal object out of his pocket and pointed it at the petrified animal.

A noise sounded across the field, like the crack of an axe hitting wood, as Azalea skidded to a halt at the cow-bull's side. A small stick-like object protruded out of his neck.

Carefully, as the bull quickly calmed, she removed the stick and stroked the tiny wound it had left on his skin. The old cow-bull turned his head. His eyes became glazed and cloudy like sea-crystals. Azalea placed the palm of her hand on his cheek, but his legs buckled and his body slammed into the ground, where he stared up at her through unblinking eyes.

"What've you done to him?!" she cried, snarling at the Enforcement as they tried to move closer. "What've you *done?!*"

"It is just a **sedative**," said Parvan, rising unsteadily to her feet. "It is to make the bull sleep. That creature is a dangerous animal."

Azalea could feel the blood pumping through her veins.

"He's not sleeping, he's *dead!*" yelled the girl.

The Sapien female walked over to look at him.

"The sedative should not have been strong enough to kill it," she said, inspecting the old cow-bull's body from a distance. "It must have been ill. It must have had a heart-attack or something."

"He weren't ill," growled Azalea. "He was old." Her parents were suddenly there at her side, as Parvan signalled for the Enforcement to take the old cow-bull away. "What're you doing?" cried the girl, tears now pouring freely down her face. "Where are you taking him?"

Aspen placed a trembling hand on the back of her neck.

"There's nothing we can do for him now, Azzy." He looked at his daughter with pleading eyes. "We need to get on with our work. Do you understand?"

She went to protest but could not find the energy.

"Is this how it's going to be from now on, Pa?" she asked, and without answering, he took hold of her hand and led her back to the trench.

136

When the earth-millipedes had trailed out of the hole to find a new home, shovelling earth became a welcome distraction from her furious thoughts. But Oak-Lea had no such task to take his mind off the terrible news. His legs were not strong enough for digging and Azalea found him at the roots of her tree when she arrived home later that lightness, his cheeks stained with tears.

"You've heard."

The boy nodded.

"My pa died to save the old cow-bull," he said, quietly. Azalea held his gaze with her own for a long moment. He almost managed a smile in response. "Some of the Farnorthern Villagers came down to harvest, so I asked if they'd lay him to rest near the marsh-pond. It was the nicest spot I could think of. I haven't been there yet. Will you come with me?"

The smell of burning lavender drifted along the grassway as they approached the water. Flowers had been laid in intricate patterns on the broken earth and some of the villagers had made a fire next to the graveside. The two friends sat on the edge of the pond for a long while, neither possessing the words to explain how this felt.

Azalea's parents had also come to pay their respects. As Oak-Lea headed back out to the grassway, they placed some flowers on the grave and told Azalea it was time to go home.

"Can I stay a bit longer?" she asked. "Just for a while?"

Her mother stroked the back of her head.

"Don't be long," she told her.

Azalea pulled a section of moss from the log, positioned it on top of the soil and pushed an acorn into it. A white crow-hen alighted on a nearby branch. It tilted its head with interest, as a flow of tears dripped down the girl's face.

"I'll never forgive them for this," she said. "Never," and the aching in her chest roared like fire, as the crow-hen took flight and disappeared into the darkening sky.

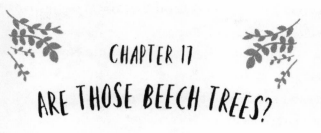

CHAPTER 17
ARE THOSE BEECH TREES?

The energy-house was built in seven lightnesses. The Sapiens brought barrows of orange bricks through the Gateway and assembled them into a hideous lump of a building, with no windows and only one door. It was almost as if it had sprung up from the ground like a fungus and rooted itself in Azalea's world.

Inside the building, tiny parts of a large mechanicary had been pieced together, and a metallic shell was constructed outside. Parvan said it would expand their world, but Azalea thought it was nothing more than an eyesore. She had seen the Sapiens testing the mechanicary near the grassway, where the shiny monstrosity moved across the land as if having a life of its own.

Oak-Lea had been asked to assist with assembling the components. He sat all lightness in the dingy energy-house, twisting strands of metal and sticking them together with glue. He said he enjoyed it, but

Azalea did not see how anyone could enjoy being shut away in a box all lightness.

As for Azalea, she hated the stupid energy-house. In fact, she swore if Parvan asked *her* to work in there too, she would refuse to do any work at all. But for now, her task was to dig yet another trench.

This one was long and thin. It started at the energy-house and stretched out across the landscape like a waterless stream, until reaching the grass-meadow on the northern side of the forest. The Sapiens called this piece of land the New Village. They had already started to lay the foundations of several homes and many more temporary huts had been set up nearby. Azalea squirmed at the thought of this strange species living so close to her tree.

"I'll be able to see them from my sleeping-hut," she told Bryony one lightness, as they walked towards the Farnorthern Hills. "It's going to be awful."

"At least you don't have to look at *his* smug face every lightness." The girl signalled to someone on top of the hill. Rowan Vine was strutting around on the grass like a red-chicken. "He thinks he's better than the rest of us, just because he knows a few Sapien words. He's such an embarrassment."

They approached the top of the hill, where a small group of Homotium were waiting and three Sapien boys were carving a shape from a fallen tree-trunk.

"You're late," said Rowan, as they joined the others. "You were told to arrive at **midday**."

Bryony grunted.

"Perhaps if you used proper words, we'd know when we're meant to be here."

"Everyone else knew," he told her. "It means when the sun is directly overhead."

"Why didn't you just say that then?" muttered Azalea.

The boy clapped his hands to draw the group's attention. It was clear he enjoyed the power that came with being part of the Vine family.

"When the Sapiens have fixed those **propellers** to that post," he said, "you can use the rope to pull it upright. You'll need to dig a hole in the ground first to stand it in." *More digging,* thought Azalea, *that'll make a nice change.* "Any questions?"

Azalea squinted into the sunlight for a better view of the objects. They looked a bit like giant sycamore seeds.

"Yes," she said, "I've got one. Are those made out of beech trees?"

"I meant questions about what I've asked you to do," he replied. "Not general ones about stuff you don't know."

141

Azalea pursed her lips.

"Only, the huts in the New Village are made out of beech wood as well," she went on, "and there's a herd of grass-deer who come into the forest during winter. They eat the beech-nuts to survive."

"Well, this wood didn't come from Midpoint Forest," said the boy, "so don't worry about it. Wait here a *minute*, everyone, while I check if the propellers are ready."

Bryony folded her arms into sharp points as he walked away from the group.

"I can't believe I'm related to him," she sniffed. Azalea could *totally* believe it, but she didn't say so. "I don't know how much longer I can put up with him bossing me around without telling him to get lost."

"Hello."

The voice surprised them. They turned to see the Sapien boy they had met on the other side of the Gateway standing in front of them. His hair stood neatly on end and two small seeing-windows were perched like a mistle-thrush on the bridge of his nose. The boy held an empty hand out towards them. Azalea scowled as if having been offered a wet jelly-squid, and the boy looked embarrassed before shoving it back in his pocket.

"I am Mason," he smiled. He paused, as if expecting

142

some kind of response. "Do you have a name too?"

Azalea lowered one eyebrow.

"Obviously," she replied.

Mason scuffed his foot on the grass.

"I was upset about your cow-bull," he said, as if having plucked the words out of thin air. "It was a terrible thing that happened."

"Why would *you* be upset about it?" asked Bryony. "You never even knew him."

"Well, no," said Mason. He chewed at his cheek. "I just meant I am sorry for your loss."

"He en't lost," said Azalea, "he's dead. The Enforcement killed him." Then she nodded towards the propellers. "Haven't you got some carving to be getting on with, pal?"

She watched with disdain as he scurried back to his work.

"What a dung-beetle," muttered Bryony.

"I thought the Sapiens are meant to be dangerous," said Azalea. "I mean, I know he helped us on the other side of the Gateway, but that one don't seem like he's got the brains to be dangerous."

Something caught her eye in the valley below.

"The propellers are almost ready," said Rowan, walking towards them. "Come and start digging so we can get this thing upright."

"Where are *they* going?" asked Azalea.

A large group of Homotium from the Farnorthern Village were walking south through the dale. Rowan glanced down at them.

"The Sapiens are building a mechanicary pathway through here. Quite a few places in the north will need to be flattened to make way for it."

"What's that got to do with anything?" asked Bryony.

A chill shuddered its way down Azalea's spine.

"Those beech trees, please tell me they didn't come from the Farnorthern Village."

For a moment, the tiniest glimmer of guilt appeared on Rowan's face, but he quickly corrected it.

"They won't need their trees anymore," he said. "They're going to live in the New Village."

Bryony stared at her brother in disbelief.

"You cut down their trees? We thought those huts had been built for the Sapiens to live in. Homotium can't sleep on the ground, Rowan, it's not natural, and the grass-meadow is too close to the Crystal Shore. They'll be living right next to the mud-lizards. I can't believe you let the Sapiens do this."

"They'll be fine," he said. His eyes turned to the group from the Farnorth then back to Bryony. "They'll get used to it."

"They shouldn't *have* to get used to it," snapped Azalea. "At least let them live in Midpoint Forest with us. There's plenty of space."

The boy instantly shook his head.

"The huts have been built now, and the Sapiens said—"

"Oh, well, if the *Sapiens* said it, we'd better make sure we do it," mocked Bryony. "Fields forbid we upset the Sapiens. I know, why don't we ask their permission?" and she put two fingers in her mouth and whistled. Mason and the other Sapien boys turned. "Azalea wants to ask you something!" she called over to them.

Azalea shoved Bryony hard on the arm, but Mason was already walking towards them. He brushed the sawdust from his hands.

"Azalea," he said. "That is a nice name. What is it you wanted to ask?"

The girl attempted a smile but it felt more like a grimace.

"You see those Homotium down there in the valley? They're from the Farnorthern Village. Your people cut down their trees and now they're expected to sleep on the ground with the mud-lizards. Can't they just live in Midpoint Forest instead?"

The boy raised his shoulders.

145

"I do not see why it should be a problem. But the houses we are building will be more comfortable to sleep in than a tree."

She looked at the boy as if confused by his very existence.

"Have you ever slept in a tree?"

"No, but—"

"Have you seen a mud-lizard smash through a boulder with the flat of its skull?" Mason's eyes bulged like grey-pigeon eggs. "No, thought not. That's settled it then – they're moving into the forest."

"Actually," he told her, "I will have to check with Parvan. But I am sure she will see how important it is for the Homotium to live in their natural habitat."

Bryony laughed at the ridiculousness of that statement, but his words made the hair on the back of Azalea's neck stand on end. She took a step forward and peered down her nose.

"Did you just say, our *natural habitat?* We en't marsh-beetles, you know."

"No, of course not, sorry, I just..." He did not back away, but he looked like he wanted to. "It will be fine," he told her. "I shall make sure of it."

Parvan's consent was given later that lightness. Azalea was furious at having to ask for it, but she sat in the lavender field for a long while after and the buttermoths eventually calmed her temper. The Farnorthern villagers had collected wood for the new tree-huts. Azalea helped to cut and assemble them, and by sunfall they had built almost twenty new homes. It was tiring work, and as darkness fell she collapsed into her bed with exhaustion.

At first, Azalea was only vaguely aware of the rustling at the roots of her tree. She sat up, pulled open the window-shutter and poked out her head. A female Homotium from the Farnorthern Village was rummaging through the brushwood, her thick auburn hair obscuring her face.

"Is there something you need?" Azalea called down to her. The female jumped, dropping her handful of hazel-nuts onto the ground. "I'm sorry, I didn't mean to scare you. It's just, you don't need to forage during darkness. We have plenty of food if you want some."

"Thank you," the female replied, her voice barely audible. The moonlight snuck through the branches and lit her face as she picked up the seeds. "I have enough now though. Sorry to wake you."

"I've seen you before," said Azalea, "at the plum-berry orchard. I was having an argument with this girl I know. You probably don't remember."

"I do," she replied, walking away from the tree.

"Are you settling in all right? It must've been

147

horrible having your tree torn down like that. I'm Azalea, by the way."

The female pushed her hair to one side.

"Tulipa," she said, no louder than a bird's twitter. "Tulipa Birch," and with that, she scuttled away into the forest.

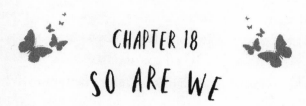

CHAPTER 18
SO ARE WE

Azalea overheard her parents talking from outside the living-hut doorway.

"I just can't see an end to it," said her mother. "When I agreed to join the alliance, I didn't realise it meant living like this. They're controlling us, Aspen. I've got a right mind to tell Ceanotha she can shove her alliance where the sun don't shine." Aspen smiled. "What?"

"It's nice to have the old Marjoram back," he said.

"Yes, well, those Sapiens bring out the bad side of me, that's all."

The early sunlight trickled in through the open window-shutter as Azalea entered the room and helped herself to a bowl of oats.

"If we hate them being here so much," she said, "why don't we do something about it?"

"You shouldn't be eavesdropping," said Marjoram.

"I weren't eavesdropping, you're just loud, that's

all." She raised both eyebrows at her mother. "Anyway, I don't reckon the Sapiens are as dangerous as Ceanotha makes out. There's this one boy who's about as dangerous as a field-mouse."

"I suppose we could ask them to dig their own holes once in a while," said her father. "My hands are sore from all that shovelling."

"Or we could just tell them to do one," mumbled the girl.

"Azalea!" scolded her mother. "That's not polite."

"I didn't think we were worried about being polite no more, Ma."

Aspen placed his bowl onto the table and unhooked a harvesting bag from the wall.

"We need to bide our time," he told them. "I hear the Sapiens are planning to cross the ocean to visit the distant land. With a bit of luck, they'll decide to stay there."

"That's nonsense," said Marjoram. "They'll never build a bridge long enough and the mud-lizards will eat them alive if they build a raft. Grab a harvesting bag, Azalea, we're going to the potato-field. We need to collect as much food as we can before Parvan finds us more jobs to do."

Oak-Lea and his mother were also making their way through the forest.

"How's things, Marj?" asked Rosa-Lea, without her usual cheer.

"They've been better," she answered. "I was just saying to Aspen, I've got a right mind to tell Ceanotha where she can shove her alliance."

Rosa-Lea's face lit up like a fire-fly's tail.

"Marj! You're back!"

Marjoram grimaced.

"Why does everyone keep saying that? I'm just angry about the old cow-bull and I'm angry about what happened in the Farnorthern Village. Imagine coming home one lightness to find someone had chopped down your tree. It doesn't bear thinking about, does it?"

Oak-Lea became unusually animated.

"Lilian said it was the worst thing that ever happened to her," he told them. "She said the Enforcement just turned up and shouted everyone down from their trees. They weren't given a chance to pack up their things or nothing."

"How terrible," said Aspen, shaking his head.

"Poor things," agreed Marjoram.

"Blasted Sapiens," his mother remarked.

Azalea crinkled her nose.

"Who the heck is Lilian?"

"Oh, she's the girl Bryony sometimes hangs out

with from the Farnorth," he said. "We got talking while the huts were being built last darkness."

"Well, it's a shame *Lilian* wasn't helping us build instead of standing around talking to people she barely knows." Azalea stopped as she reached the grassway and squinted into the sunlight. "Is that her over there with Bryony? Why are they standing outside the energy-house?"

Seeing Oak-Lea, the girl called Lilian smiled and the boy smiled back. It was clear she had arranged to meet him there. Azalea looked the other way. In the distance, a group of Sapiens were felling trees at the side of the restricted woodland. Ceanotha and Thornton were there too.

"For fields' sake," muttered Marjoram. An old sycamore crashed to the ground. "There won't be any trees left at this rate."

As her parents headed towards the scene, Azalea followed Oak-Lea to the energy-house. When they reached the hedgerow, a movement drew her eyes to the west. Someone was hiding amongst the flowers in the lavender field. Tulipa Birch was crouched low in the stems, watching the Vines with interest.

Bryony followed Azalea's eyeline to the mass of hair poking out through the buds.

"Lilian, isn't that the weird female from your

village?" she asked. The girl obediently nodded. "I suppose we should feel sorry for her really. I mean, what sort of a Homotium lives on their *own*?"

"Lots of Homotium live on their own, Bryony," said Azalea. "Your grandmother lived on her own before your father—" She almost said 'died.' "Before your father left."

"Yes, but Tulipa Birch lived *completely* alone. Tell her, Lilian."

Azalea gave Oak-Lea a sideways glance. The look on his face said this promised to be the most fascinating story he had ever heard in his whole entire life.

"Well," said the girl, her voice like that of a young sky-robin, "she was born to a nomadic couple on the edge of the Eastern Cliffs, and when they died, she stayed there all by herself. She's only lived in the Farnorthern Village for the last few seasons."

Before Azalea could respond, a familiar voice flew over the fields. She turned to see her mother yelling at a group of Sapiens and Tulipa Birch vanishing unseen into the lavender.

"YOU CAN'T *DO* THAT!" she cried. "HAVEN'T WE GIVEN UP ENOUGH FOR YOU ALREADY?"

Without hesitation, Azalea ran towards her. A cloud of buttermoths swarmed up from the lavender, as a group of Sapien workers sliced the stems with a curved tool.

"What's happening?" she panted. Her father was holding her mother's hand to stop her running into the field. "Why are they cutting the lavender?"

"The mechanicary pathway is being built through here," he told her. "They're going to dig up the whole field."

"OVER MY *DEAD BODY!*" bawled Marjoram.

Azalea had never seen her mother lose control like this. It was both magnificent and terrifying at once.

"Go home, Marjoram," Ceanotha said, calmly. "I shall make sure the lavender is carefully bundled and shared out amongst the village."

"If you think I'm going home while you let these creatures tear down our world—"

"They are not *creatures*," snarled Ceanotha. "They are an intelligent people with knowledge and ideas."

"SO ARE *WE!*" bawled Marjoram.

The old female signalled to Parvan. Several Enforcers ran over. Aspen pushed Azalea behind him and took hold of Marjoram's hand.

"Ma, please, stop," said Azalea. "Someone's going to get hurt."

"Azzy's right," agreed Aspen, "you have to calm down. We can grow more lavender but there's only one Marjoram. Let's go to the potato-field like we planned."

Azalea's legs felt weak as they walked away from the lavender. The sound of stems being cut came from behind her but she didn't look back. She could not take her eyes off her mother's face.

"We've got to do something," said the girl. "We can't carry on like this."

The lines of her father's face appeared both angry and broken at once.

"You're right," he replied, his voice unfaltering. "We'll hold a meeting this darkness in our living-hut and come up with a plan. Just a few of us so Ceanotha doesn't get wind of it." He placed an arm around his daughter's shoulder. "Don't worry, Azzy," he told her, "I won't rest until this land is ours again."

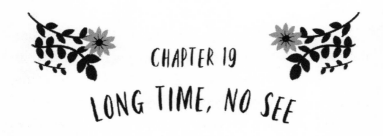

CHAPTER 19
LONG TIME, NO SEE

When the harvesting bags were full, a band of heavy storm-clouds blew in from the other side of the ocean. Azalea walked through the red-poppy field. The lavender had been stacked in the New Village and the scent of cut stems perfumed the air as she swerved the sand-dunes near the Crystal Shore.

The first heavy raindrop fell as she lifted four of the bundles into her arms. Azalea was unaware of anything else as she stood in front of the flowers, but gradually she realised she was not alone. There were people living in the temporary huts of the New Village. An old Sapien female was watching Azalea through a clear window, but she closed the shutter as their eyes met.

A voice sounded nearby. Mason was playing on the grassland with his sister. The girl squealed as he chased her around the hut, but seeing Azalea, they stopped.

"Hello," he smiled. "You remember my sister? She

is Mabel."

The girl ducked behind his legs, peeping out through big eyes at the towering Homotium in front of her. Azalea snapped a stem of lavender from the bundle and held it out towards her.

"Do you remember me?" she asked. "This is for you. You can take it."

Mabel stepped out from her hiding place. She looked up at her brother, then back to Azalea. Then she took the lavender and brought it up to her nose, before joining a group of Sapien children who were playing a game on the grass.

Azalea watched as they jumped over a long strand of twisted rope, not caring about the rain.

"Are your family living here now?" she asked Mason.

"My mother and sibling have just arrived," he said, "and my grandparents will follow soon." His eyes turned to his sister. "It is good to be in a world that is safe. On the other side of the Gateway, we lived behind a wall to keep out the predators. We did not see them often, but we always knew they were there."

"It must've been a relief when the Gateway reopened," she said.

"I suppose so. It happened just after I was born, so I have never known any different."

The boy's mother appeared in the doorway of the hut. She recognised Azalea and walked towards her, an awkward look on her face.

"He-llo." The female's voice was loud and slow, as if Azalea might not hear her otherwise. She pointed at herself. "Barbara. How do you doing?"

Azalea was not sure what any of that meant, but she smiled and nodded, and Mason's mother seemed happy with her response. She said something to her son in their own language, then she called Mabel's name and the girl ran to the hut.

"We have to eat now," said Mason. "Do you want to meet together next lightness? Your friend has helped build the mechanicary and I am teaching him how to **drive** it. You can come with us if you like."

"No, thanks," blurted Azalea. She hadn't meant for that to come out quite so carelessly as it did. "What I mean is, I'm really busy. You know, holes to dig and... Well, holes to dig. See you around," and she hurried towards the forest.

The rain poured through the trees like waterfalls as she ran towards home. Every Homotium she passed was carrying as much lavender as they could hold while they rushed to get out of the rain, some balancing it on their shoulders and others dragging it behind them in small carts.

Nearing the new homes of the Farnorthern villagers, Azalea saw Tulipa Birch climbing her tree empty-handed.

"Tulipa!" she called up into the branches. The female looked down in surprise. "Don't you want any lavender?"

"It's all right," she said, "I have some sticks. I can use those instead," and she resumed her climb.

"I think what the Vines are doing to us is terrible," Azalea added. Her words caught Tulipa's attention and the female stopped climbing. "I saw you watching them earlier from the lavender field and I could tell you were thinking the same thing."

Tulipa looked as if she might say something, but then changed her mind.

"Listen," Azalea went on, lowering her voice, "we're having a meeting this darkness. It's only a few of us, so don't tell anyone else. We're going to think up a way to stop the Sapiens ruining our world. You can come if you want."

"No," she said. "I can't. Sorry."

"If you're worried about leaving your tree during darkness, it's okay. The meeting's going to be held in our living-hut and it en't far. My family live literally four trees over there and you're unlikely to see a mud-lizard so far inland."

"I can't." Tulipa pulled her hair over her face, almost falling in her urgency. "Tell Aspen I'd like to, but I have things to do," and she shot up into the leaves.

*

When Azalea was back in her tree and the storm clouds had blown over the Eastern Cliffs, darkness seeped into the forest like a fog. Oak-Lea and Rosa-Lea were the first to arrive for the meeting, then a knock sounded on the wall of the living-hut. Lilian walked in with her parents. Azalea pouted as she entered the room. She didn't know *she* had been invited, but Marjoram said it was important to involve both Homotium villages.

"So," began Aspen, as the group sat down on a circle of mats, "I've had an idea. From what I've heard, about sixty Sapiens have come through the Gateway so far. The first families arrived this lightness and soon there'll be hundreds, possibly a thousand more of them. But what if we cut them off at the source?"

"You mean the Gateway?" asked Rosa-Lea. "'Ow are we gunna do that?"

"We could seal up the hatch," suggested Oak-Lea.

"Oh, yes," said Lilian, "that's a super idea."

"Yeah, super," mocked Azalea, "until the Sapiens who're already here go and *un*seal it. We'll have to come up with something better than that."

"We should stand up to the nasty beggars," said Rosa-Lea, "tell 'em what's what. We should arm ourselves with sticks and rocks, and force 'em back through the Gateway like they forces us to dig them 'oles."

"As much as I'd like to do that," said Marjoram, "we could all end up with a sedation stick in our neck if we put up a fight."

Lilian's mother cleared her throat.

"We could try talking to Parvan," she said, her voice as delicate as a buttermoth's wing. "If we explain how sad all of this is making us feel, she might listen. Shiitake believes there is kindness and understanding in everyone."

"Shiitake?" sniggered Azalea. "What's that?"

Lilian's father timidly raised his hand.

"It's me," he said. "My mother named me after her favourite mushroom," and now Azalea openly guffawed in his face, before realising he was serious.

"Oh," she said, composing herself. "That's...nice."

"I think it's a brilliant name," said Oak-Lea. He offered Lilian a smile. "I wish I had a cool name like that."

"Shiitake Moss?" scowled Azalea. "You'd sound like a foot fungus." She looked at her mother. "I reckon Lilian's ma is right about talking to them, but Parvan might be the wrong Sapien to choose. She's part of the Enforcement and they don't seem to listen to no-one."

Her mother was staring into the fire, lost in her own thoughts.

"What if the other end of the mechanicary house tunnel had collapsed instead of the one in the ruins?" she said. "They couldn't have come through the Gateway at all if it was buried under the ground."

Before anyone could answer, a subdued howl came from the roots of the tree. The Homotium looked at each other with wild eyes. What if Ceanotha had found out about their meeting?

Azalea volunteered to see who it was, then climbed to the lowest branch and looked down through the darkness.

"Tulipa? I thought you weren't coming."

"I wasn't, but I've had an idea. Is Bryony with you?"

"No, we didn't tell her about it in case her grandmother got suspicious. It's just a few of us, but you'll know Lilian and her parents from the Farnorthern Village. Oh, and you've met my pa before."

The female froze.

"Have I?"

"I guess so. You mentioned his name when we spoke earlier. Come on up and I'll introduce you to the others."

They climbed to the top of the tree, where the group were waiting in silence. Azalea stepped through the grass doorway and Tulipa followed, her hair flopping over her eyes as she turned her face to the floor.

"It's all right, everyone," Azalea said, "it's just Tulipa. I invited her earlier on. She won't tell no-one."

The room studied the new arrival. Tulipa looked up. She pushed her hair away with the back of her hand, peering out from beneath it like a frightened field-mouse.

The faces of Azalea's parents dropped, as Rosa-Lea stood slowly up from her mat.

"Well, I'll be ploughed," she breathed.

"Hello, Rosa," said Tulipa, nervously. "Long time, no see."

Marjoram's jawline tightened, but Aspen started to smile.

"I don't believe it. Is it really you?"

"You can see it's her, Aspen," snapped Marjoram, "and I don't know why you're so surprised. We've already seen one Vine come back from the dead this season, so this is *exactly* the kind of trickery we've come

163

to expect from that family."

"Marjoram, please," said the female, "I can explain."

"You'd better," snarled Azalea's mother, "because I'll bet my last lavender-bunch you've got something to do with the Sapiens coming to our world." She turned to her daughter. "Azalea, your friend's name isn't Tulipa Birch. It's Primrose Vine."

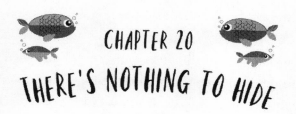

CHAPTER 20
THERE'S NOTHING TO HIDE

"You're Bryony's ma?" scowled Azalea. "But you told me your name was Tulipa."

"I know, I know," gabbled the female, "and I'm sorry. You must think I'm a terrible person for abandoning my children like that, but I had to leave, I had no choice." She took hold of her hair with both hands, as if it was somehow keeping her afloat. "When Ceanotha told me about the Gateway, I was scared for my life and I was scared for the lives of my children. I thought it would be best for everyone if I left."

"You knew about the Gateway and you didn't tell anyone?" gasped Marjoram.

"I couldn't. Ceanotha said we would all be in danger if the village found out. She said I had to go through the Gateway and form an alliance with the Sapiens, but I told her I wasn't going to live in another world, I was going to stay here with my children and she'd have to find someone else to build the alliance.

That's when I got sick. You remember me getting sick, don't you?"

"Of course," said Aspen, "and when you disappeared, we all thought you had died. We assumed Ceanotha had invented the story about you leaving to spare the feelings of Bryony and Rowan."

Primrose's chin quivered at the sound of their names.

"Ceanotha had been making soup to build up my strength. It tasted strange, like nothing I'd ever eaten before, and I seemed to feel worse after drinking it. I confronted her and she told me I knew too much. She said I wasn't loyal to my family and she didn't trust me not to tell the whole village about the Gateway. She said the existence of the Sapiens was to be kept a secret at all costs and if one Homotium must be sacrificed for the safety of the others then—"

"So be it," finished Aspen.

Marjoram shot him a look from the corner of her eye.

"She poisoned you too, didn't she," said Oak-Lea, and the female nodded.

"That darkness, I somehow managed to climb down from the tree and drag myself away from Midpoint Forest. I found shelter under an old hazel tree near the Eastern Cliffs and I honestly thought I would not survive the darkness. But I did, and I spent the rest of that summer eating fallen hazel-nuts and drinking dew from a small clump of cherry-grass, until autumn came and I found I could stand."

"Is that when you came to the Farnorthern Village?" asked Lilian's mother.

"No, this was a long time before that," replied Primrose. "I thought about going to your village, but I was worried Ceanotha would find me there, so I travelled further north instead."

"More lies," sneered Marjoram. "You can't go further north than the Farnorth, Primrose – the clue's in the name. Not unless you're expecting us to believe you swam across the ocean to the distant land," and she snorted her amusement.

Primrose looked at them through eyes like moons.

"You didn't!" gasped Rosa-Lea. "But the mud-lizards nest on the Crystal Shore, Primrose. You could've been eaten."

"Fear can make people do things they wouldn't normally consider," she said. "If I'd been thinking straight, I would never have done it."

"What's it like?" asked Azalea. "The distant land, I mean."

"It's much like ours. You can see the Crystal Shore from the coastline. I'd watch it from my tree at sunfall

167

and think about my children. Until one lightness, I couldn't stand the separation any longer and I decided to come home."

"So now we're expected to believe you swam the ocean *twice?*" scoffed Marjoram.

"No, I built a raft the second time. It still wasn't an easy journey to make, but I waited until the water was calm and paddled as little as possible so as not to attract the lizards. No-one in the Farnorthern Village was familiar with my face, so I made-up a story to explain who I was and kept myself to myself." Primrose smiled. "I would often walk south to visit the orchards and watch my children from a distance."

Azalea's father scooped a cup of hot berry-juice from a pan without taking his eyes off her face.

"Being separated from them must've been so difficult for you," he said, passing her the drink.

Marjoram snatched the cup from his hand and slammed it down on the table, spilling the contents all over the floor.

"I don't expect it was very nice for her children either!" she snapped.

"You're right," said Primrose, "I was selfish, I know, but I was so frightened, Marjoram, and I wasn't thinking straight, I was just—"

"*You were just thinking about yourself!* If you'd told us

168

about the Gateway all those seasons ago, Oak-Lea wouldn't have been poisoned and the Sapiens might not be here in our world. You could've stopped all of this, Primrose, but instead you just hid behind that stupid hair of yours and did nothing."

"I'm sorry, Marjoram, really I am."

"Don't pretend you came here to apologise. The only reason you came here is because you knew one of us would recognise you eventually. You thought it would look better to confess than to be found out." Marjoram paused as another thought entered her head. "Or did Ceanotha put you up to this? Did she send you here to spy on us, is that what this is?"

"No!" wailed Primrose. "Ceanotha doesn't know I'm alive and she mustn't find out! I won't be safe if she knows!"

"But she's got no reason to hurt you anymore," said Azalea. "Everyone knows about the Sapiens, so there's nothing to hide now."

Primrose scratched at her scalp, her hair ruffling into a tangled mess.

"I shouldn't have come here," she flustered. Her face was grey and her neck was blotched with hot red patches. She turned to Azalea's mother. "I'm begging you, Marjoram, *please* don't tell Ceanotha you've seen me," and with a final glance towards Aspen, she ran

169

from the hut.

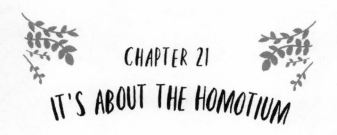

CHAPTER 21
IT'S ABOUT THE HOMOTIUM

The sun woke to a cloudy sky. Azalea cleared yesterlight's ashes from the fire-pit as her mother opened a window.

"Don't be fooled by all that crying and wailing and wafting of hair," said Marjoram. "Primrose Vine has always been an attention-seeker, hasn't she, Aspen?"

"Be fair, Marjoram," he answered. "She hasn't exactly had much attention for the last forty seasons. She's been on her own in the distant land."

Marjoram whipped her head like a spinning sycamore seed.

"Why must you *always* take her side, Aspen?"

Azalea's father screwed up his face as if a horrible smell had just entered the room.

"How am I always taking her side? I haven't seen her for forty seasons."

"If you're going to feel sorry for anyone," Marjoram

went on, "you should feel sorry for those poor children. Imagine growing up without parents and then both of them coming back from the dead in one season."

A burst of laughter escaped from Azalea's mouth.

Her mother glowered.

"Sorry," said the girl. "It just sounded a bit funny."

"Well, it's *not* funny, Azalea. Didn't we have enough going on without Primrose Vine turning up and throwing her hair into the mix? And I suppose it'll be *our* job to tell Bryony and Rowan she's still alive."

Aspen looked up from his breakfast.

"You can't tell them, Marjoram. It's up to Primrose whether or not she wants to tell her children, not us."

"There you go again, taking her side."

"I am *not* taking…" He took a deep breath and lowered his voice. "I'm not taking her side. I just think we should stay out of the Vine family's business."

While her parents continued their debate, Azalea went to meet Oak-Lea at the side of the marsh-pond. The scent of over-ripe fruit hung in the air like smoke, the reflection of the trees rainbowing the surface of the water.

Azalea dived through the colours and resurfaced amongst a shoal of striped-mackerel, as Oak-Lea rested his walking-sticks on the moss-covered log.

"So," she began with a grin, "what do we think about Primrose Vine being alive?"

"I think it's terrifying," he said. "How many more Vines are gunna come back from the grave?"

Azalea pulled herself onto the bank and the boy sat down next to her.

"Before she came up to the living-hut last darkness, Primrose told me she'd had an idea. Then my ma frightened her off before she could tell us. I wonder what she was going to say." Azalea shrugged. "Are you working at the energy-house this lightness?"

"Yes. Do you wanna come and see the mechanicary?"

"Why does everyone keep asking me to look at the stupid mechanicary?" she asked.

"I just thought you might be—" He lowered his eyebrows. "Who else has asked you to look at it?"

"One of the Sapien boys keeps talking to me. He said he's been teaching you to..." She thought for a long moment. "I can't remember the word he used."

"Oh, you mean Mason. He's teaching me to drive."

"Yes, well, I don't reckon we should be making friends with the Sapiens, Oak-Lea. It feels like we're excusing all the changes they're making, not to mention the way they're ordering us around all the time. I have to flatten out the lavender field this

173

lightness and if I'm friendly to the Sapiens, they'll think I'm okay with it and I en't." Azalea stood up on the bank. "Actually, I think I'm going to visit Primrose before I start work. We never *did* come up with a plan last darkness and I reckon there might've been more she wanted to tell us."

A rancid smell drifted along the grassway as Azalea headed back to the forest. A group of Sapien workers were heating a black mixture near the lavender field. It smelt unnatural and caught in the back of her throat, as she held her breath and quickened her pace.

At Primrose's tree, Azalea climbed to the living-hut without howling, stood outside the doorway and cleared her throat.

"Who's there?" Primrose called from inside.

Azalea parted the grass and walked in.

"It's only me. Sorry for not howling. I didn't want my ma to find out I was here."

There was a large bag near the door. Azalea couldn't see what was in it, but it was too big for harvesting.

"I've just been at the marsh-pond with Oak-Lea," she said, conversationally. "He was telling me about that awful mechanicary the Sapiens have built. One of them's teaching him to drive it apparently and—" She suddenly realised the room was practically empty. There were no bowls, no mats, no drying towels near

174

the sink and the pile of sticks Primrose used for the fire was strangely small. "Sorry," said Azalea, "but are you going somewhere? Only, all your stuff seems to be in that bag."

Primrose clasped her hands together and twiddled her fingers, biting her bottom lip at the same time.

"I'm leaving," she said. "I can't be here when your mother tells Ceanotha. I'm going to spend this lightness gathering food, then the following sunrise I'm heading back to the distant land."

"But you can't leave again. Midpoint Forest is your home and you shouldn't let Ceanotha control you like this. Who cares if she finds out? She's got no reason to silence you anymore and no right to threaten you. In fact, I reckon once you tell everyone what she did, it'll be *her* who'll want to move to the distant land."

Primrose smiled.

"You remind me of your mother." Azalea was not sure how to take that. "Sit down," she said, "I've got something to tell you," and Azalea perched on the edge of the table, looking out through the open window to the side of the New Village. "Have you noticed how the Sapiens are scared of us, Azalea?"

"Some of them, yes," she replied. "I don't know why though. There are loads more of them than there are of us."

"It's because they know something you don't. Ceanotha knows too. She told me many seasons ago and I didn't believe it at first. But I know now for certain it's true." The reflection of the fire came to life in her eyes. "If I tell you, will you promise to keep it a secret until I am gone?"

"Of course," she said. "Is it about the Sapiens?"

"No," replied Primrose, "it's about the Homotium."

CHAPTER 22
I'LL BE HOME BY DARKNESS

By the time Azalea reached the lavender field, the other Homotium were already there. Some of the Sapiens were flattening the ground with stone rollers and others were still stirring up the foul, black fluid in big metal containers.

Azalea was asked to take the mixture to the other end of the field in a wheeled barrow, where she would pour it onto the ground for the other Homotium to even-out with rakes. It was a long and tedious task, and Azalea grew bored of it quickly.

As she tipped out her twentieth barrow, her parents and Rosa-Lea began spreading it over the ground.

"I've had an idea," whispered Marjoram, checking the four of them were alone. "It won't get rid of the Sapiens who are already here, but it would stop the others arriving." She paused, her eyes scanning the area for eavesdroppers. "I think we should *bury* the Gateway."

Azalea put down her barrow.

"That's a joke, right?"

"The other end of the tunnel has already collapsed," her mother explained, "so with a little help from our digging-spades, the same thing could happen in the woodland." Rowan Vine was watching them with curiosity. "We'll discuss it later," hissed Marjoram, as he started to walk over.

The boy stopped in front of Azalea.

"You're supposed to be fetching more **tarmac**." He pushed a stray curl from his eyes. "Parvan wants the mechanicary **road** to be finished as soon as possible, so you shouldn't be standing around chatting, Azalea."

"It's no worse than standing around *not* chatting like you're doing," she replied. "And if Parvan's so keen to get this thing built, why doesn't she try helping us for a change?"

Rowan puffed up his chest.

"I'm supervising," he said, "and Parvan is teaching some of the other Homotium how to move building materials through the Gateway. In fact, you should be down there too. All younger females are required for the lifting work. Did you arrive late this lightness and miss the **briefing**?"

Sighing, Azalea left her parents and headed towards the restricted woodland. A pathway had been cleared through the trees to make way for the new road, so she walked miserably between the severed trunks until reaching the hatch.

A Sapien girl, not much older than Azalea, was standing next to the entrance. Several Enforcers were scattered amongst the trees, staring in her direction.

"Do not worry about them," said the Sapien girl. "They are always here to guard the Gateway. They are a bit annoying, but they will not bother you." She smiled widely. "Is your name Azalea?"

"How do you know that?" she asked.

"I am friends with Mason. My name is Charlotte. We look after the children of our village together in the **evenings**. We go to the sand-dunes to tire them out before sleep."

"You shouldn't do that," Azalea told her. "The dunes are dangerous. They're too close to the Crystal Shore and that's where the mud-lizards nest."

"Thank you for your advice, Azalea. We have not seen any lizards yet, but we shall be careful from now on. If you would like to meet us one evening and join our game, you would be most welcome. It will be good for the younger children to make friends with a Homotium."

Azalea noticed the girl's cheeks had tiny dents in them, as if someone had prodded her with a cooking-poker on both sides of her face.

"I'm not allowed out of the tree during darkness," she told her, "but thanks for inviting me." Azalea peered down the hatch. There was a rope dangling into the hole. "Sorry, what is it I'm meant to be doing exactly?"

A Homotium girl from the Farnorth climbed out of the hatch. She pulled the rope and hauled a basket of black stones to the surface, loaded them into a barrow and pushed them towards the lavender field.

"We are bringing rocks through the Gateway," said Charlotte. "If you climb down, Parvan will show you how."

The Sapien leader was waiting at the bottom of the tunnel when Azalea ducked out of the hole. Bryony was there too, and the Sapien leader was explaining how to move through the Gateway.

"I've done it before," said Bryony, as Azalea entered the chamber. "And I know how to hold rocks, thanks."

A familiar drone filled the chamber as Lilian fell out of the light and onto the floor, dropping her container in the process. She glanced at Bryony, then hurriedly picked up the stones and scurried into the tunnel without so much as a smile.

"Hello to you too," frowned Bryony. "What's *her* problem?"

Azalea shrugged. It seemed she had not heard about her mother yet, and she guessed that was why Lilian was avoiding her.

"Let's go together," said Azalea, then she took hold of Bryony's wrist and stepped into the light.

On the other side of the Gateway, a Sapien male was awaiting their arrival. He showed them out of the building and onto the patch of grass at the centre of the village. Some other Homotium girls were loading containers with small black rocks from the back of a mechanicary, but Azalea's eyes were drawn to the distant skyline, where a huge grey wall towered around the buildings.

"It must've been awful living inside that wall all the time," she said to Bryony, pointing between the tower-blocks.

"Yeah, well, now *we're* the ones living in fear," she muttered, "so don't pity them too much, Azalea."

The two girls filled their containers while the Sapiens who were still living there stared down at them from the surrounding windows. They heaved the stones towards the building before carrying them into the light, where they drifted through time like leaves on the ocean.

Azalea landed at somebody's feet when she fell through the other side of the Gateway. It was

Charlotte. She was there in the place of Parvan. The girl held out her hand to Azalea and helped her up from the floor.

"The pulling-rope has snapped," she said. "Parvan has gone to find another. She said you may go back to the wheeled barrows until a new one is found."

Azalea put down her container and climbed up to the hatch, to the sound of Bryony complaining about the rudeness of the Sapien in the chamber.

"Who does she think she is?" snarled the girl, as they walked between the severed trunks of the missing trees. "*You may go back to the wheeled barrows.* Thanks for giving us your permission, but we do have minds of our own, you know."

"Her name's Charlotte," said Azalea, "and I don't reckon she meant it like that. She doesn't know our language very well yet."

"Oh, my fields," gasped Bryony, "did you just use a Sapien word?" and Azalea scowled as they headed out of the woodland.

Her parents were near the grassway. Azalea saw them from a distance, but suddenly, as she moved closer, she realised there were two Enforcers holding her mother's arms.

"She hasn't done anything wrong, Ceanotha!" Aspen shouted, as Azalea hurried towards them. "She thought the digging-spades would work better than the rakes, that's all. We were going to use them to flatten-out the tarmac."

"It's all right, Aspen," said Marjoram. Her voice was calm but her eyes were desperate. "Let's not make this worse than it already is."

Parvan came over from a neighbouring field.

"This Homotium has been stealing," the old female told her. The way in which she referred to Marjoram by species suggested she was an animal or an insect. "She took five digging-spades and hid them in that laurel-bush over there."

Ceanotha looked sternly at Marjoram then talked to Parvan in the Sapien language. It was the first time Azalea realised how fluently she could speak their words. They chatted for a short moment, nodding their heads and lowering their voices. Then Ceanotha turned back to Azalea's mother.

"Parvan agrees we must set an example to the other Homotium," she said. "You must learn that actions have consequences, Marjoram."

"She's not a child," snapped Azalea's father.

"Aspen, *please*," urged Marjoram.

The Enforcers started leading her towards the woodland.

"Wait, where are they taking her?" he asked.

"To the mechanicary house," Ceanotha replied. "She will remain there for the rest of this lightness as a punishment for her behaviour."

"You can't do that!" cried Azalea, directing her anger towards Parvan. "You've got your stupid spades back, so just let go of my ma!"

Several Enforcers leapt in front of her, putting themselves between the Homotium girl and the Sapien leader.

"Azalea," said her mother, her voice breaking, "get on with your work. It's just a building. I'll be home by darkness," and with a final nod, Azalea watched helplessly as her mother was taken away.

CHAPTER 23
DON'T YOU FORGET IT

Azalea did as little as possible for the rest of that lightness. She pushed the barrow lazily and loaded it with half the amount of tarmac it could hold, then waited as long as possible before starting the task again.

The sun moved slowly over the sky, but the moment it touched the ocean Azalea dropped her barrow and wandered towards the marsh-pond. She sat at the old cow-bull's grave, drawing patterns in the broken soil with the end of her finger, as Mason appeared from the grassway.

He seemed surprised to see her.

"Sorry," he said, "I came to look at your marsh-pond, but I can leave if you like," and he turned back to the grassway.

"It en't *my* marsh-pond," said Azalea. The boy stopped. "You can stay if you want."

Mason sat down on the moss-covered log. He

watched with interest as a black and white fish streaked across the surface of the water.

"What type is it?" asked the boy.

"A striped-mackerel. You often see them near the top of the water because that's where it's warmest." Azalea wondered if she should ask about what happened to her mother, but before she could decide, she had already spoken the words. "Why did they do that to my ma?"

Mason's cheeks turned crimson.

"I am sorry for the actions of my people," he said. "They say we should be scared of the Homotium, but I do not understand why." He looked into the water. "I sometimes wish I was a fish, then I could swim to the distant land and get away from the fully-growns of my species."

Azalea wanted to smile, but stopped herself.

"When are your grandparents arriving?" she asked.

"In a few lightnesses." The boy suddenly remembered something. "I am meant to be helping my mother set up their new home. They are both old, so we want everything to be ready for them. I had better go. Shall I see you on the next lightness, Azalea?"

"Oh, well, I...I can't. I have to brush my hair. It's really, erm, tangly."

"Okay," he said. Azalea could see he wanted to

laugh but was trying not to. "I shall see you another time then," and waving his hand, he left the pond.

She stayed a little longer to watch the striped-mackerel enjoying the last glimmer of sunlight, before walking back to her tree. The living-hut fire had extra lavender fuelling its flames and her father had prepared the supper, but her mother still wasn't home.

The grass of the doorway didn't move until the forest was fully dark. Aspen hurried over to her as she wearily entered the room.

"Don't make a fuss," said Marjoram, tiredly. "I'm all right."

"Did they hurt you?" asked Azalea.

"Of course not. I was fed and watered and perfectly safe, but I feel a bit...broken."

Aspen clenched his teeth and breathed heavily through his nostrils.

"Well, it won't happen again," he seethed. "They had no right to treat you that way, Marjoram. The less Sapiens we have in this world, the better. I think we should go ahead with your plan."

The look they shared made Azalea feel empty inside.

"Why don't we try talking to the Sapiens first before we go burying the Gateway?" she said. "They're not all like the Enforcement. Some of them are actually all

187

right once you get to know them."

Marjoram looked at her through bloodshot eyes.

"How can you say that after what they just did to me?"

"Sorry, Ma. I just think if we could—"

"What? All live together in peace and harmony? All just get along? What do you think we've been trying to do, Azalea? The fact is, no matter how much we give, they'll always want more."

"But burying the Gateway would mean splitting up families and friends. That's not what you want, is it?"

"They weren't worried about separating *us* when they locked your mother in the mechanicary house," said Aspen. He handed Marjoram a bowl of food. "In fact, they seemed pretty pleased with themselves about it."

"Not all of them," she said, quietly, but her parents chose not to hear her.

"I know you're trying to help, Azzy," he said, "and I know you're scared, but I promise we'll make this better. Why don't you take that food to your hut? Me and your mother need to talk about this. It's almost bedtime anyway. Eat your food and then get some rest, Azalea."

A ball of anger swelled in her chest as she picked up her bowl. He'd might as well tell her she was too young to say anything useful, so she climbed down to her sleeping-hut in furious silence, where she stared out of the window-shutter and across the land.

The moon lit the water of the Great Western Beach. Azalea felt she could almost reach out and touch it, but the walls of the hut pressed in on her, restricting her freedom. The sound of laughter came from the New Village. Mason and the other Sapien children were playing outside in the darkness. She remembered Charlotte asking her to join them. Then she got to her feet, moved to the doorway and stood quietly for a long moment.

She shouldn't go. It was dangerous near the Crystal Shore and her parents would be worried if they found her room empty. But she doubted they'd leave their conversation to check on her, so she left the hut and scrambled quietly down to the ground.

At the edge of the Sapiens' village, a cluster of lights danced over the sand-dunes. Mason sensed Azalea's dark-vision on the back of his head and turned. He was holding a bright object, as if having plucked the starlight down from the sky.

"Azalea! You are here!"

"Yeah," she said, embarrassed by his enthusiasm. "What's that?"

"It is a **torch**. We all have them. Come and meet

189

everyone."

The girl scanned the area for lizards before following him onto the sand, where a group of younger children came over to greet her. The darkness felt safer now she wasn't alone.

Mason's sister was there, and Charlotte too. Their cheeks were flushed, as if they'd been running. Once Azalea had been introduced, one of the boys pointed his torch at the girl next to him, who squealed with excitement before running across the dunes. The others extinguished their own lights and did the same thing, shouting and laughing as they scrambled up the sandy slopes.

"What're they doing?" asked Azalea.

"That boy is chasing them," explained Mason. "If he catches them with the light of his torch, they are out of the game. The last person left is the winner."

The beam swept across the dunes towards them, narrowly missing their heads. Azalea ducked.

"Should I hide?" she asked.

"Yes," he grinned, "it is every Sapien and Homotium for themselves!" and placing the torch into his pocket, he ran over the sand.

Azalea could not extinguish the light from her eyes so easily, so instead she peered through her fingers as she made a run for the biggest dune. She was much faster than the Sapien children and flew up the slope like a rock-gecko, skidding to a halt between two small coconut-trees.

Someone else was already hiding behind one of the trunks. It was a girl, slightly younger than Azalea. They looked at each other with uncertainty and then, "Hello," whispered the girl.

Azalea smiled.

"Hi," she said.

The two girls watched from their hiding place as the beam of light found each of the other children in turn, until only the two of them were left in the game.

Forgetting her dark-vision, Azalea peered out from the trees. The silvery light of her eyes flooded the dunes and the boy with the torch spun around to look at them. The Sapien girl giggled. She pulled Azalea back behind the tree, said something in Sapien then jumped to her feet, as the boy with the torch started running towards them.

Azalea laughed and stood up, but a movement in the shadows caught her eye. A female mud-lizard slid over the top of the dune and stopped in front of them.

The Sapien girl saw it and whimpered.

"Keep still," hissed Azalea. She took hold of the girl's arm. "Don't move."

The other children saw the lizard from the bottom

of the slope and started to panic.

"Take them back to the village," she said to Mason. "Go slowly and stay quiet."

Mason spoke softly to the group, ushering them away from the sand, as the Sapien girl's breath trembled in the back of her throat. Tears streamed down her face as the creature sniffed at the air.

"Do you speak Homotium?" she asked. The girl gave a tiny nod. "What's your name?"

"B-Bethan."

The mud-lizard jerked its head. Bethan's arm flinched, but Azalea tightened her grip. Then the creature gave a low grumble as it paced towards the trees. Its back quarters were wider than usual.

"Bethan," said Azalea, "this lizard wants to lay her eggs under these trees, so we're going to move out of her way. But we must do it slowly and quietly."

"R-run," she stammered.

"No," Azalea said, quickly, "mud-lizards are much faster than…" She almost said 'you'. "They're much faster than us, so we're going to get a head-start by walking backwards to the bottom of the dune and *then* we can run."

Gently pulling the Sapien girl's arm, Azalea took one careful step backwards. Bethan moved too. They took another, then paused, and then another, and the mud-lizard snorted the wet from its nostrils. The suddenness of its action made Bethan cry out, and the creature's eyes flared suddenly yellow as it tipped back its head and roared.

Without thinking, Azalea grabbed Bethan by the waist and hoisted the girl onto her back. She ran down the bank of the dune with the mud-lizard close behind her, as Mason appeared on the other side of the sand.

"Run!" she shouted. *"Go into your hut!"* and by the time he had reached the wooden building, Azalea had caught up with him and they burst through the door together in a frantic state, slamming it closed behind them.

Gasping, Azalea put Bethan down on the floor. Mason's mother gathered her up and held the girl as she cried. Then Azalea went to the window and peered through the slats of the shutter. The mud-lizard was pacing the ground outside.

"They don't like noise," she said, still trying to catch her breath. "That's why we stay away from them. I shouldn't have left the tree during darkness. I don't know what I was thinking."

"It was lucky for us that you did," said the boy. "Thank you, Azalea. We had the wall to protect us from predators on the other side of the Gateway, and here it seems we have you."

"I saw the wall earlier this lightness. Your people must've been really frightened to build something like that." She looked out of the window. The mud-lizard was nowhere in sight. "I'd better go," she told him. "My ma's going to go nuts when she finds out about this, by the way, so I reckon we should stay away from those dunes from now on."

"You know more than my species realise, Azalea," he said.

"That's right, pal," she grinned, her eyebrows high on her forehead, "and don't you forget it," and with a final check through the window, she headed back to her tree.

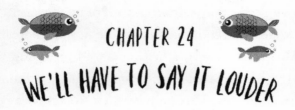

CHAPTER 24
WE'LL HAVE TO SAY IT LOUDER

Oak-Lea was inside the energy-house when Azalea arrived the following lightness. He was sitting at a table, fiddling with small metal objects, but turned with surprise as she entered the room.

"What're you doing here?" he asked. "Aren't you supposed to be working on the road?"

"You wanted to show me the mechanicary," she said, "and I felt bad for saying no, so, here I am. We can go for a drive, or whatever it is you call it."

The boy's face came to life more than she had ever seen it before. He rose from his chair and picked up his sticks.

"I've been desperate to show someone," he said. "I en't good enough to drive on my own yet, but Mason will be here soon. Let's wait outside."

Azalea could see her reflection in the golden shell of the mechanicary. A long seat had been built at the front and there was an open space in the back, where the

195

Sapiens loaded stones or sand or whatever else it was they wanted to move from one place to another.

Azalea climbed in and Oak-Lea sat next to her.

"This is a **steering-wheel,**" he told her, "and those are the **pedals.** One of them makes it go and the other one makes it stop, and the wheel lets you choose which direction you want to travel in."

Azalea noticed a panel in front of him.

"What are those?" she asked.

"**Buttons,**" he said, as if this explained it. "I don't know what all of them do, but this one's my favourite. I'll show you in a bit."

Mason walked around the side of the energy-house. Seeing Azalea, he clapped his hands and punched the air for no particular reason.

"I *knew* you wanted to see the mechanicary!" he cheered. "I just *knew* it!"

Oak-Lea laughed, but Azalea gave him her most severe look as he climbed onto the seat next to her.

"I did not *want* to see it," she told him. "I'm Oak-Lea's friend and he was excited about it, so… Anyway, I can't believe the fully-growns are letting the likes of you two drive their precious mechanicary."

Oak-Lea twisted the corner of his mouth.

"Well," he said, "they don't exactly *know* about it."

It was Azalea's turn to laugh.

"Oak-Lea Moss, don't tell me you've been doing something you en't allowed to do? Aren't you worried about what my ma will say?"

"She won't say nothing if she don't find out," he answered. "Oh, and there en't no need to be scared of the noise. It's just the **engine**."

"What noise?" she asked, and with a push of a button, the mechanicary roared into life.

Azalea's heart almost burst from her chest. She looked at Oak-Lea, then she looked at Mason, and then she laughed harder than she had for a very long time.

"I knew you'd like it," said Oak-Lea.

The boy placed his foot on the pedal and the mechanicary lurched forwards. Azalea's back pressed into the seat as they sped away from the energy house, bumping and jolting over the fields as if they were riding in a kangaroo's pouch.

Before reaching the red-poppy field, Oak-Lea turned the wheel. The mechanicary left the grass and moved towards the Great Western Beach, where it slid down the shingles like a giant sea-snail.

"Not many Sapiens who are my age have learnt how to drive," said Mason, "but my grandmother is a **mechanic**, so she taught me when I was small."

Azalea realised they were heading towards the water.

"You'd better turn that wheel thing," she said, "or we're going to end up in the ocean."

Oak-Lea grinned.

"Are you ready to see what my favourite button does?"

He reached out a finger and touched one of the circles, as the wheels splashed into the shallow waves. Something big and grey burst out from around the casing, bulging like a puffer-fish's belly. Azalea grabbed hold of the seat and prepared to jump out through the window, but then, as the front of the metal giant crashed into a wave, she realised something incredible.

"How…how is this thing *floating?*" she gasped.

As they moved further across the ocean, the girl gazed back to the shore of the land she had never left until now. The pebbles looked like gravel from so far away and the grains of sand had morphed into a singular stretch of yellow. Her world had always been beautiful, but suddenly the sight of it stole her breath away.

She looked in the other direction. Sunlight silvered the ocean like the skin of a rainbow-carp and Azalea felt tiny in its hands. A male rock-puffin circled above her, the white of its belly blurring against the blue of the sky as it swooped towards the water. Then a fish darted up from the surface. It soared over the front of the mechanicary as if riding the ocean air before slipping back into the water.

"Wait," said Azalea, "did that fish just...fly?"

"You can't see them from the shore," said Oak-Lea. It was the first time he had ever known more about fish than Azalea. "So we think the flying ones only live out here in the deeper water."

Mason pushed open a window in the roof of the shell, one Azalea had not noticed until now, and they stood on the seat with their heads out in the open air. The breeze pushed her hair back off her face, the spray of the ocean cooling her skin, as a shoal of fish arrowed out of the waves.

"Do you want to see the cliff-falcon nest too?" asked Mason. "The babies have just hatched."

Azalea knew her voice would sound emotional if she spoke, so she simply nodded instead, as Oak-Lea steered the mechanicary towards the White Rocks.

A tangle of sticks sat on one of the ledges, expertly woven and padded with moss. A large bird stood at the side of it, a black hood covering its head and hooked toes curling over the stone. Inside the nest, Azalea saw three speckled chicks. Their feathers were woolly like rabbit fur and their beaks were open. The cliff-falcon called once, looked out across the ocean then took to the sky, where its shadow fell over the mechanicary as it searched the waves for fish.

Directly above the nest, there was an opening in the rock. Azalea squinted up at it, shielding her eyes from the sunlight to see someone had painted a picture on the flat of the stone. It looked like a drawing of two figures. Oak-Lea spotted it too, she could tell by the look on his face, but then the distant land caught Azalea's eye from behind the rock-face.

"Can this thing get all the way over there?"

"Perhaps," replied Mason, "but we must not go further than this. We shall get into trouble and it could be dangerous."

Azalea looked at him for a long moment.

"Don't you want to find out what's over there?" The tone of her voice had changed. It was flatter and less friendly, as if accusing the boy of a terrible wrongdoing. "Or do you already know?"

Oak-Lea laughed nervously in the brief silence that followed.

"Why would Mason know about the distant land, Az? We can't drive all the way over there because we need to get the mechanicary back to the energy-house before the other Sapiens notice it's missing."

The awkwardness lingered as they headed back to the shore. Oak-Lea made polite conversation, then

Mason muttered his goodbyes as he left the mechanicary and Azalea started towards the new road.

"Hang on," said Oak-Lea. He stood in the doorway of the building. "What was all that about?"

"What?"

"You suddenly being weird with Mason."

Azalea sighed. Then she walked back to where he was standing and lowered her voice.

"I visited Primrose yesterlight and she told me something about the distant land. If I tell you, do you promise not to tell anyone else?"

Suddenly, Lilian charged around the corner of the energy house, her face red and her eyes frightened.

"Have you heard?" she asked, breathlessly. "The fully-growns are going to bury the Gateway."

"Bury it?" gasped Oak-Lea. "How?"

"By using the digging-spades to make the ground above the chamber collapse," said Azalea. "It was my parents' idea. I didn't think they'd actually go ahead with it though. Who told you about this, Lilian?"

"My father. He said most of the Homotium fully-growns think it's a wonderful idea and they're going to do it next darkness. What if the ground collapses from under them? Or what if the Enforcement hear about it? Somebody could get hurt."

Azalea shook her head in dismay.

"This all has to stop," she said. "I don't want to live in a world like this."

"But what can we do?" asked Oak-Lea. "We're just children."

A fire lit up in Azalea's heart. She wasn't *just* anything.

"Lilian, you gather the children from the Farnorthern Village, and Oak-Lea, you get the children from ours. The young Sapiens don't want none of this either, so I'll talk to Mason and get them onside too. Parvan is bound to find out about this, so we'll go to the woodland and talk some sense into *both* species, whether they like it or not. We'll need as many voices as possible though if we want them to listen, so do your best to get all the Homotium you can."

"And what if the fully-growns won't listen to us?" asked the boy.

Azalea shrugged.

"We'll have to say it louder, I suppose."

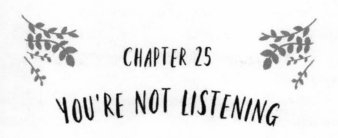

CHAPTER 25
YOU'RE NOT LISTENING

"Well, that's just great, isn't it," huffed Marjoram, throwing the remains of her burnt breakfast into the flames. "Why does everything seem to go wrong lately?"

"You didn't stir it enough, Ma, that's all. Don't worry though, I'll make you some more." Azalea took the pan from her mother. "You were probably too busy thinking about what's happening later on."

Her words were as pointed as Flora Elm's nose.

"How do you know about that?" snapped Marjoram. "I specifically told the other villagers *not* to tell their children. We all agreed you're too young to worry about this. Was it Rosa-Lea?"

"No, and I *am* worried, Ma, because it's a stupid idea."

"Azzy," her father said, sternly, "don't talk to your mother like that."

"But it's true, Pa. I mean, how are you going to make

203

the earth above the chamber collapse without falling down there yourselves?"

"For your information," said Marjoram, matter-of-factly, "we've made ropes." She snatched the pan back from Azalea. "We're going to tie one end to a tree and the other around our waist."

"Wow, that sounds safe," mumbled the girl, rolling her eyes. "You do know it won't cave-in just because you want it to, right? That chamber's been there for thousands of seasons and the ceiling en't fallen down yet."

"No, but all the other ruins have, so I doubt it'll take much encouragement."

"Well, what if the Enforcement are there? They're always watching the hatch."

Her mother threw the pan into the sink with a clatter.

"There are only two of them there during darkness. By the time they've alerted the others, it'll be too late."

Azalea growled with frustration.

"You've thought of everything, haven't you," she spat.

"Yes, thank you," replied Marjoram.

"Everything except *me!*"

Her mother's face looked as if someone had stamped on her foot. She grabbed a cloth and scrubbed at the pan, punishing it for having the cheek to burn on the same lightness as she was burying the Gateway.

"Of course we've thought of you," she said. "The whole reason we're doing this is *because* we've thought of you. We can't live like this forever, Azalea."

"But how are we meant to live with the Sapiens who are already here once you've separated them from their families? It's going to be worse than ever." She turned to her father. "Tell her, Pa."

Aspen looked wearily at his daughter.

"One step at a time, Azzy," he said. "We'll deal with the consequences when and if they happen."

"MARJORAM! MARJORAM, COME DOWN HERE!" There was no mistaking the shrill voice of Flora Elm. She was standing at the roots of the tree, shouting up into the branches. "HURRY UP, I'VE GOT SOMETHING TO TELL YOU!"

Marjoram and Aspen exchanged confused looks as they left the hut. Azalea followed them to the forest ground.

"If this is about Rosa-Lea's hair again," sighed Marjoram, jumping down from the trunk, "you'll have to take it up with her, Flora."

"No, it's better than that," she replied. Her face was the most excited Azalea had ever seen it. "The mechanicary's gone missing. Someone's taken it."

205

"Well, we didn't think it had crawled off on its own," muttered Azalea.

The female lowered her voice, despite having already told half the village the very same news.

"I know who it was," she hissed. "I heard a noise on the forest ground last darkness, so I looked out of my window. Something big was scuttling around in the moonlight and then I realised...Tulipa Birch was standing at the roots of Rosa-Lea's tree." Azalea grew suddenly interested. "She threw a rock into the branches and somebody climbed down the trunk. Then the two of them disappeared into the darkness and they didn't come back again."

Flora Elm's eyes stuck out from her face as if growing on stalks, then she nodded to signal the end of her story.

"And?" said Azalea's mother. "You're not suggesting Rosa-Lea stole the mechanicary, are you?"

"Oh, come on, Marjoram, we all know what she's like. I didn't get a very good look at her, but if the cap fits—"

"Oi!" Rosa-Lea stormed towards the tree. "En't no-one told you it's rude to talk about folk behind their backs?"

The female's smile melted.

"Rosa-Lea. I didn't see you there. I was just saying

to Marjoram —"

"I 'eard what you was just sayin', but I didn't steal no mechanicary, Flora. I reckons you must've been dreamin'."

"Well, no, I—"

"So why don't you potter off back to your tree and keep your big nose out for once?" Flora Elm froze in a stunned silence, until Rosa-Lea added, "Or do you need the toe of my shoe to 'elp you along the way?" and the female scooted into the trees like a rabbit.

Azalea started to laugh, but then Rosa-Lea turned to Marjoram with urgency in her eyes.

"Can I come up?"

"Of course. What's wrong?"

"Not 'ere," she said, and they climbed back up to the living-hut.

"Is it Oak-Lea?" asked Azalea, as they entered the room. "Is he sick again?"

"He didn't come up for 'is breakfast earlier on," said Rosa-Lea, "so I checked 'is sleepin'-hut and he en't there neither."

"Perhaps he went to the energy-house at first lightness," suggested Aspen.

Rosa-Lea shrugged.

"Or perhaps he's nicked the Sapiens' mechanicary." The boy's mother started to pace the floor. "He's been learnin' to drive it. He only told me about it yesterlight. One of the Sapien boys has been teachin' 'im and now it's gone missin', so I reckon he's the only Homotium what *could've* stolen it."

The blood drained from Azalea's face. Why hadn't she realised it before?

"You're right," she said. "It must've been Oak-Lea that Flora Elm saw leaving the tree last darkness."

"But why's he done it?" his mother asked. "And why was he meetin' Primrose? If the Sapiens find out, they'll lock 'im in the mechanicary 'ouse."

"You're jumping to conclusions," said Marjoram. "Perhaps one of the Sapiens took the mechanicary and Oak-Lea's already at the energy-house like Aspen said. Let's go and check before we start panicking."

But Azalea had already started to panic. She hurried through the forest, trotting along next to them and trying not to let the worry show on her face.

"You won't be able to go ahead with your plan now," she said to her mother, "not if Oak-Lea's missing. You'll have to cancel, or at least postpone it."

"There en't no need for that," said Rosa-Lea, her face steely. "Those Sapiens are the reason my Oaks is missin', so you stick to your plan, Marj and make sure that Gateway's good and buried."

The feeling of panic grew in Azalea's chest.

"But Oak-Lea wouldn't want—"

"That's enough, Azalea," Marjoram said, as they neared the energy-house. Parvan and the Vines were chatting outside the doorway. "It doesn't look like he's there. Let's act like everything's normal and tell them he's ill or something. We can go to work on the mechanicary pathway and quiz the other Homotium about it, see if they know where he might've gone," but Azalea had the sickening feeling she already knew.

After watching the three of them walk to the energy-house, Azalea collected a wheeled-barrow from the edge of the woodland. At the southernmost side of what had once been the lavender field, Mason was mixing tarmac in a metal container.

When he saw her approaching, the boy stopped stirring and glanced at a nearby group of Enforcers.

"Did you hear about the mechanicary?" he whispered. Azalea nodded. "Was it Oak-Lea?"

"Yes, and one of the other Homotium has gone with him too. She was planning to run away to the distant land. I reckon Oak-Lea has taken her there."

"His actions have made the Enforcement suspicious," said the boy. "Parvan thinks this might be the start of a rebellion." Azalea was confused. "Some of the digging-spades have been taken too," he explained. "They suspect your mother has something to do with it, because of what happened before, so they are keeping a very close eye on her. They think she is preparing your people for battle."

"A battle? No, of course not. There *is* a plan though, a really dangerous one. A few of us are doing our best to stop it happening, but we'll need lots of voices if we want the fully-growns to take any notice. Can you convince your friends to meet us near the woodland at sunfall?"

A member of the Enforcement called over to Mason. The boy picked up his stirring-stick and resumed turning the mixture.

"Yes," he said, "but you must go now. That Enforcer is getting suspicious. We shall meet you there, Azalea," and with a quick nod, she picked up a barrow and left.

Azalea could think of nothing but Oak-Lea as she wheeled the tarmac that lightness. She kept looking towards the ocean, expecting to see him floating back towards the shore, but as the sun lowered into the Great Western Beach he had still not appeared.

Azalea trudged towards the forest and went back to her tree, the knot in her stomach tightening as her parents' plan grew closer. They ate their supper in silence, then Marjoram threw more lavender on the fire to keep it burning whilst they were out, and before Azalea knew it was happening, the sunlight started to fade.

"Stay here and wait for us to come back," instructed her mother. "You're not to leave this tree, Azalea Fern, do you hear me?" and they were too distracted to notice she promised nothing, as they took their digging-spades and went to the woodland.

Movement busied the forest as the other fully-growns came out of their trees to join them. Azalea could hear their footsteps from her living-hut, so she waited until they were gone before going to the roots of her tree.

Lilian was the first to arrive, followed by the children of the Farnorth and then those from Azalea's own village. It seemed Oak-Lea had convinced many of them to add their voices to the cause before he had left and Azalea wished he was standing there next to her now.

As they started towards the grassway, someone shouted her name. She turned to see Bryony rushing towards her.

"I thought I'd missed you," puffed the girl.

"I didn't think you were coming," said Azalea. "Didn't your grandmother notice you leaving?"

"She's not there. She stayed in the woodland with Parvan when we finished working. Rowan and my father are there too. That's what I've come here to tell you. They don't normally stay there this late."

"They must know what my parents are planning to do," breathed Azalea.

"Maybe," said Bryony. "But if they *don't* know, my family could be in the hatch or on the other side of the Gateway when they…"

As her sentence trailed off, Azalea saw the fear in her eyes. A first glimmer of dark-vision flickered over them. Azalea nodded, and then she sped through the forest, the rest of the children trailing after her.

Mason was at the side of the woodland. His sister was there and Charlotte too, plus several more Sapien children from the New Village. Seeing the urgency on her face, he waited for her to speak first.

"My parents have gone to the hatch with the other fully-growns. They've got the digging-spades and they're going to bury the Gateway."

It was Mason's turn next.

"I have just seen many Enforcers leaving the New Village. They were heading towards the woodland. There is going to be trouble, Azalea, I am sure of it."

The girl drew in a trembling breath.

"We need to stop them," she said.

They pelted through the trees as one group, no-one caring about the brambles or nettles. As they neared the hatch, they followed the sound of hushed voices and found Marjoram tying a rope around another villager's waist. Many other Homotium fully-growns were there too. Their dark-vision lit the faces of their children in the gloomy woodland.

"Everyone, stop!" cried Azalea. Marjoram looked over her shoulder. She eyed the young Sapiens who were standing next to her daughter. "We don't want you to do this. It's going to make things worse."

"Azalea, what're you doing here," said her mother, "and why are you with those Sapien children?"

"It's okay, Ma, they're on our side. Your problem isn't with them, it's with Parvan and the Enforcement. These children don't like the way we're being treated either. The Enforcement want to control our species because they're frightened of us. If you bury the Gateway, you'll prove they're right and they'll just be even more scared than they already are."

"They're not *frightened* of us," spat Marjoram. She tightened the knot of the rope. "There are hundreds more Sapiens than there are Homotium, Azalea. Now do as you're told and go home, *all* of you."

A tall figure approached the clearing from the direction of the mechanicary house. The Homotium fully-growns became silhouetted by the light of Ceanotha Vine's eyes. Parvan was there too and several members of the Enforcement. Then Azalea heard the snap of a twig on the ground behind her and turned to see Thornton and Rowan with more of the Sapien Enforcers.

"You should listen to your daughter, Marjoram," said the old female, "and stop this nonsense immediately. The ground underneath us is lined with stone, so the plan your people have made is not going to work."

"*Your people?*" scowled Marjoram. "Have you forgotten you're one of us, Ceanotha?" Azalea's mother walked heatedly towards the old female. "The reason we've been forced to make such a desperate plan is because we don't know what else to do. Our world is being taken away from us piece by piece and we work all lightness to build something we don't want. Why are you letting them do this to us, Ceanotha?"

As Marjoram grew closer to the old female, Parvan spoke quietly to the Enforcers. There was a shout as one of them pulled a sedation-pistol from his belt and three others seized hold of Azalea's mother.

"Leave her alone!" cried Mason. "She does not wish to hurt you. She only wishes for us to treat her with kindness. We don't want to live this way, Parvan," and he continued to talk to her in their own language.

Azalea thought she saw something change in the

Sapien leader's expression as he spoke, but then her father stepped out from the group and the female's eyes narrowed.

"Let – go – of – my – Marjoram," seethed Aspen. Azalea's stomach turned. She had never seen anger engraved so fully in his face before. He lifted the metal end of his digging-spade over his head. "I'm warning you, let go of her, or I'll make you wish you'd never set foot on our land."

"Pa, *no!*" shouted Azalea, her eyes flooding with tears. "This isn't right! You're not listening to us!" and she closed her eyes as her father brought down the spade.

CHAPTER 26
ANOTHER DAY

Marjoram pulled her arm free and shielded the Enforcer, as the end of the digging-spade dropped towards him.

"No, Aspen!" she shouted. The metal spade stopped no more than a breath away from the Sapien's head. "You've never hurt another living thing in your life, Aspen Fern, and I won't let you start now. This is *not* who you are."

He threw the tool onto the ground, his arms hanging limply down at his sides.

"I don't know what else to do," he said. "How are we meant to protect ourselves if we don't fight back?"

Azalea ran to him and took hold of his hand.

"This isn't the only way to fight back, Pa," she told him.

A noise drifted in from the west. Everyone fell silent as they turned to face it. It sounded like voices, *lots* of voices, and it was coming from the Great Western

Beach.

Azalea scanned the faces of the children from her own village. She thought of Oak-lea and Primrose, and then, without words, she let go of her father's hand and ran towards the grassway.

"Wait," called Bryony, as she and the rest of the children started to follow, "where are you going?"

"To the beach," she replied.

From the top of the shingles, they looked out across the moonlit ocean. The voices were louder here, singing an unfamiliar song in a strange language, and something was moving across the water near the cliff-face. It drifted steadily over the gleaming surface, as the roar of an engine joined the chorus and the mechanicary came into view.

"It's Oak-Lea!" shouted Azalea. "I knew it!"

Bryony squinted across the rolling waves.

"Not *just* Oak-Lea," she said, pointing into the distance. "Look."

A fleet of smaller vessels emerged from behind the White Rocks. The mechanicary was towing them on long ropes, fiery torches lighting their way. As they drew nearer, groups of figures became visible on each one of them, then a female stood up inside the mechanicary, her head sticking out from the top of the casing and her thick hair blowing back off her face in

217

the salty sea air.

"Primrose is still with him!" cried Azalea, the joy of seeing her friend still fuelling her excitement. "She came back to help us! Do you see her?"

She turned to Bryony, realising she had spoken her mother's name without thinking.

The girl frowned.

"You mean *Tulipa*," she said.

Parvan and the Enforcement ran onto the shingles, with Azalea's parents and the other Homotium following close behind. Ceanotha stormed to the front of the group.

"What's going on?" she fumed. She spotted the mechanicary and the female inside it. "Who *is* that?"

Azalea's joy beamed out of her face like starlight.

"It's Primrose Vine," she announced, loud enough for the whole group to hear, "and she's told me why she grew sick all those seasons ago, Ceanotha. It's because you poisoned her like you poisoned Iris Green."

Thornton's face turned grey. Then his top lip curled and he looked furiously at his mother.

"Is this true?" he asked. Azalea realised this was the first time he had heard the news. Ceanotha turned her eyes away from him. "How could you do that to me, to our children? She was my Primrose, she was my world."

"It's like I've told you," Ceanotha replied, coldly, "if a few lives have to be sacrificed for the good of our people, then—"

"*Don't* say it," he snarled. "I'm *sick* of hearing you say that!"

The mechanicary moved closer to the shore.

"Before Primrose left, you told her about the Gateway," Azalea went on, staring Ceanotha unblinkingly in the eye, "but you also told her another secret." The old female's face tightened. "You told her there are other Homotium who live on the distant land. *That's* why the Sapiens are afraid of us, because they know we outnumber them by a huge amount."

A gasp rose up from the crowd, as the passengers of the vessels reached the shallow waves. The light of their dark-vision illuminated the shore. Then they stepped out of their wooden floats and onto the sand, where they pushed their fiery torches into the ground to scare away the mud-lizards.

"There are thousands of Homotium across the water," Azalea told the group, her voice growing stronger with every word. "Primrose didn't believe it at first, but then she went to the distant land and saw them for herself. She even lived amongst them for many seasons."

The girl turned back to Ceanotha.

"But what I don't understand," she went on, "is why you didn't tell us about them. Parvan swore you to secrecy, because she was afraid the Homotium villages would join forces and overpower her species. But you're one of *us*, Ceanotha. Why would you help the Sapiens take over our world by lying to your own people?"

The old female's answer was unusually quiet.

"I was building an alliance to unite our species," she said, "but there needed to be trust on both sides. I kept secrets for Parvan and in return she assured me there'd be peace between our two peoples."

"This en't *peace*," said Azalea. "There won't be peace until we stop being afraid of each other. There'll be no unity until everyone's equal. And life won't be fair until we all have a voice, no matter how big or small our communities."

The Homotium left their vessels and followed Oak-Lea towards the shingles. There were at least a hundred of them, maybe more, and they smiled tentatively as they stopped in front of the group.

"You said you needed more voices," called Oak-Lea, "so we brought as many as we could find. Are we too late?"

Azalea shook her head.

"No," she said, "you're just in time."

A young Homotium girl from the distant land, no more than twenty seasons old, picked up a shell from the sand. She separated the two halves. Then she walked onto the pebbled ground, gave one half to Parvan and the other to Ceanotha, before scurrying back to her mother.

The Sapien leader looked at the gift in the light of a rising moon. She thought quietly for a moment before addressing the group.

"Let us talk more **tomorrow**," she said. "I wish to see if we can put this right," and with a small nod to Azalea, she led the Enforcement away from the beach.

Azalea's heart soared like a buttermoth as she watched her village greet the visitors from the distant land. She was still on the shingles when Mason appeared at her side.

"I did not know about the other Homotium," he told her. "Parvan lied to her own people, just as Ceanotha has lied to yours. Our thoughts have not mattered to them, but now it seems we may have a voice."

Azalea nodded then turned to look at him.

"What does tomorrow mean?" she asked.

The Sapien boy smiled.

"Tomorrow is another **day**," he replied.

CHAPTER 27
SHALL WE GO TO THE POND?

Azalea pressed a final piece of moss into the living-hut window frame. An Autumn breeze blew in through the open shutter, cooling her face and bringing with it the scent of the Great Western Beach, as her family prepared for winter by padding their home like hedge-sparrows lining their nest.

She looked north towards the New Village, where a row of houses lit the landscape like giant glow-worms. The shadows of Sapien families moved inside them. Azalea could not see their faces, but she pictured Mason's mother tucking Mabel into bed as the boy cooked supper for his grandparents in the kitchen.

To the west, the remains of the demolished mechanicary road lay in broken chunks at the side of a newly ploughed field, where seeds from the cut lavender would be planted next spring. The energy house would obscure her view of the white buds, but if Oak-Lea found happiness inside its walls, learning about mechanicaries and energy and whatever else it was he made in there, Azalea supposed she would grow to like it too.

The southern side of the island was still home to the Gateway, but its light had faded when the last Sapien arrived. Many newcomers had heard about the mud-lizards and built their homes in the woodland trees with help from the Homotium people. Their huts were lit by the energy-house and a low moon outlined their walls, as Azalea's eyes fell on the crumbling bricks of the old mechanicary house.

"You're still up," said a voice.

Azalea's mother joined her at the window.

"I was just thinking how different everything looks," said the girl, "but I suppose things are only different until you get used to them. Ma, do you think the Gateway will ever open again?"

Her mother closed the window-shutter, the light from her eyes illuminating the face of her daughter.

"It might," she said, "if it finds a reason to. Anyway, I was thinking – shall you, me and your father go to the marsh-pond at first lightness?"

"Why?" asked Azalea, wrinkling her face.

"I'd like you to show me the fish," said her mother. "What do you call those little bronze ones with the grey tails again?" and as the forest grew quiet in the deepening darkness, Azalea Fern talked to her mother until sunrise.

LEAVE A REVIEW

AND THE AUTHOR WILL REPLY TO YOUR MESSAGE!

Please leave a review for *Azalea Fern and the Last Ruin of the Extinct* **on Amazon** and help other children discover Azalea's world.

You can then **copy your review to the Llama House Children's Books website** (www.llamahousebooks.com) and the author will reply to your message! Becci loves hearing from her readers and she can't wait to read your review, but please ask an adult to help.

Thank you!

WILL AZALEA FIND PEACE IN HER NEW WORLD?

WHO PAINTED THE TWO FIGURES ON THE WHITE ROCKS?

AND WILL THE GATEWAY EVER OPEN AGAIN?

DIG-UP MORE BURIED SECRETS IN AZALEA FERN BOOK TWO – COMING SOON!

MORE BOOKS BY BECCI MURRAY

Being a super-genius isn't quite
so SUPER as you might think...

STORYQUEST

CHOOSE THE PAGE - UNLOCK THE ADVENTURE

COLLECT THEM ALL!

You'll find lots of very serious poems about really important stuff (like toenails, sausages and yaks) in this hilariously irreverent collection of illustrated poetry from children's author Becci Murray.

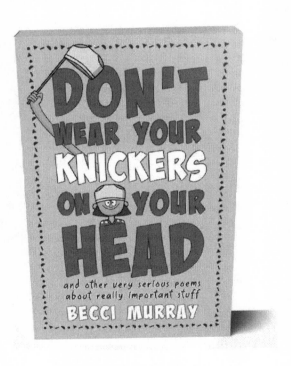

Becci Murray is a British children's author from Gloucestershire, England. She's also mum to a teenager, a chocolate labrador, a big-footed cat and a giant snail. You can learn more about Becci's books or send her a message by visiting the Llama House Children's Books website - she would love to hear from you!

WWW.LLAMAHOUSEBOOKS.COM

Made in United States
Orlando, FL
23 July 2022